ALSO BY CARMEN ROSALES

The Prey Series

Lust

Appetite

Forgive Me For I Have Sinned

Forbidden Flesh

Envy

Hillside Kings Series

Hidden Scars

Hidden Lies

Hidden Secrets

Hidden Truths

Cartel Kings Book One

Duets

Giselle

Briana

He Loves Me Not

He Loves Me

Standalone

Like A Moth To A Flame

Delilah Croww Books

Whispers in the Dark

Circle of Freaks

Erotic Quill Publishing, LLC
3020 NE 41st Terrace STE 9 #243
Homestead, Fl. 33033

www.carmenrosales.com

PREFACE

Dravin takes without consequence.

He is a sinner and never a saint.

His words drip with lust. His touch... sinful.

That is what girls whisper after one night with him. He even has the scratches to prove it.

He is powerful, dangerous, and never backs down from a challenge.

The pawn? The new girl.

He can smell her innocent nature like a piranha smelling blood and won't be satisfied until he has a taste.

The problem? He isn't the only one who wants it.

In an elite Catholic university full of lies, lust, deceit, and betrayal Gia becomes a pawn in a game of sexual seduction.

She realizes there is no one she can trust. Everything is a lie with a church full of sinners.

Dravin knows exactly what he wants though, and he won't stop until she belongs to him.

AUTHORS NOTE

Dear Reader,

The triggers include depression, death, suicide, acts of violence, and acts of bullying. All sex is for the enjoyment of all characters involved.

If you or know anyone you know that is suffering from mental health and needs help. **Please call** National Suicide Prevention Lifeline.

THIRST

Book One

CARMEN ROSALES

THE PREY SERIES

CHAPTER ONE

GIA

"THANK YOU," I tell the Uber driver as he gets in the white Honda after unloading my suitcases from the trunk.

The overcast grey clouds give off a gloomy vibe as I look at the Gothic cathedral-style building of Kenyan University. The building is imposing, and it is not just because it is a new school that I'm unfamiliar with. The campus pictures on the web are very different from what you see in person. On the internet, the images are photoshopped with the backdrop of a sunny day with a lot of green landscaping, but in reality, it looks a lot gloomier.

Kenyon University is an Ivy League school mainly for the rich. I had to transfer here just to finish my senior year because it was practically the only college that would accept me past the deadline. Some crap I read online, that they need to offer equal opportunity and allow all types of students to attend. In other words, they have spots for poor people, but they can't make it obvious that they don't want underprivileged kids to attend.

Luckily for me, even though my parents recently divorced, I still had enough for most of my tuition. The rest I had to take out in loans. My parents had to sell the house in Wisconsin to finalize their divorce. My father wanted to get it over with because he had already met someone, or rather, he had someone already from what my mother accused him of in court. The only thing I could do was get out of there as fast as I could and start my own life. Now that I'm here seeing the campus up close, it really looks like a place straight out of a horror movie. I hope this wasn't a mistake, but with my parents' drama, I didn't have much of a choice.

The smell of rain is in the air as I take out my phone and pull up a picture of the map to see where my dorm is located. The place looks deserted, except for a few people walking away from the building.

Classes don't start until the day after tomorrow. I googled the campus social media page, and from what students post about daily campus life, I see that classes here can be intense. I have decided to major in economics, and I chose a Catholic school to appease my mother. My mother is a devoted Catholic and had me attending church religiously every Sunday. It is probably why she lost it when she caught my father cheating and filed for divorce. She didn't want me to leave Wisconsin, but I couldn't deal with all the back and forth. I felt like I had to choose one parent over the other, and it was just too much. I was ready to go out into the world and become something rather than live with one of my parents. If I chose to move with my mom, my father would feel disappointed and if I chose my father, my mother would feel that I'm taking his side. In all honesty, I don't agree with what my father did to my mother, but I saw it coming. My father had been going less and less to church with my mother, and they were constantly arguing.

Throughout my childhood, the only religion I knew was Catholic. The opportunity to attend here for at least a year was too good to pass up. This religious college, built sometime in the 1800s, has a great business program. My hope is to land a good job and venture out on my own. Maybe I'll find someone to start a life with or at least date.

Hauling my suitcase, the wheels finally land on the

smooth sidewalk that crisscrosses through the trees between the buildings on the one-thousand-acre campus. The whole place looks like a maze. I pull out my phone, and a large shadow materializes behind me. I close my eyes, hoping it is just a shadow of a tree or maybe my eyes are playing tricks on me, but it's not. My shadow suddenly speaks... he speaks.

"It's that way."

My head tilts up at the sound of the sexiest voice I have ever heard. It sounds like a guy giving an interview in a sexy drawl from a late-night podcast. My eyes slowly rake up dark denim-washed jeans to a plain white T-shirt under a motorcycle jacket. He points in the opposite direction with his hand holding a black helmet. When my eyes finally land on his face, I stop and stare like a complete idiot. His eyes—they are captivating. One is dark, like midnight, and the other is blue, like the ocean.

His eyes find mine, and he raises a brow because I'm standing there staring at him like I'm dumbstruck. The man has an exotic, beautiful face with a hard, angular jaw and a straight nose. His nose is not too big or too small; it is just... perfect. His dark hair is slicked back without a piece out of place. Everything about the way he looks is just...right.

My mind catches up with my mouth, but it's too late because he turns around without saying another word.

"I-I'm—My name is Gia." I stammer, but it's too late. He keeps walking, and I curse at myself for looking stupid. "Thank you," I call out, but he continues walking, dismissing me like he never spoke to me.

My interaction with cute guys is probably a three on a scale from one to ten. I attended the University of Wisconsin for three years. My parents were strict, wanting to keep me close to home. They even kept my curfew because I was under their roof and would respect living in their house. My father obviously didn't get the memo.

I tried to date, but my mother was a devoted Catholic and was afraid I would turn into a promiscuous whore. I gave up trying to convince her that I should date and focused on completing school amid my parents' divorce my junior year. I have no problem with getting married, but the whole saving yourself for marriage thing was ridiculous. Times are different, and just because you save your virginity for marriage doesn't guarantee you will end up living happily ever after. Look at my parents. Divorced. A bunch of bullshit if you ask me. I'm tired of living the straight and narrow. It's time I spread my wings and live life.

CHAPTER TWO

GIA

AFTER I MAKE it to my dorm on the third floor, I meet my new roommate, Jesse. She likes to be called Jess and, like me, is a 'normal' student who has to take out loans to be here. She doesn't come from money. She and her mom saved just enough for her off-campus expenses for four years, and she was lucky enough to get accepted. I spent the whole day unpacking and settling in and agreed to go with Jess to a popular bar close to campus the next day.

We enter a bar close to campus the next day like we agreed. Jess seems nice and offered to hang out which I can appreciate.

"So, what is it like to attend Kenyan?" I ask Jess, taking a sip from my vodka and cranberry.

She slides her curly hair away from her face and leans slightly over the wooden table in our booth in front of me. "Different. The students here are not like other students in other universities. The majority of people that go here come from wealthy families—the elite. They are rich, and most of them have no issue showing it and reminding people like us that we are broke charity cases. Basically, if you have money, you can get away with a lot of things."

Placing my drink down over the coaster, my eyes watch as the glass sweats. Drops of water slide down the cup like rain hitting a windowpane, and the coaster soaks up the drips like I'm soaking up everything she says about this place and the people who attend. She said they get away with a lot. Now, I'm curious to know what a lot entails.

"What kind of things?"

She shrugs and scrunches her nose at me. "I don't kiss and tell. What I will do though, and only because you are my roommate, is tell you who is important and who you should stay away from."

She is about to tell me when the front doors of the Babylon bar open. The light from outside filters in, creating a bright glare that makes me squint my eyes. After a few seconds, when my eyes adjust, I see seven people coming inside—one of them I recognize from yesterday.

He walks in with an air of confidence. All the women seated at the bar eye him appreciatively as he makes his way inside. My stomach twists into knots as I remember every angle of his face from the first time my eyes took him in.

His eyes are like the shallow and deep end of an ocean. The light eye is the shallow part of the clearest water and the other one is dark like the depths of the sea. His dark hair is longer on top and faded on the sides. The man is beautiful to look at. I googled mismatched eyes yesterday when I got into my dorm because I was bored trying to fall asleep. Even with my screen cracked on my phone, I was able to read about the condition and how you could be born with heterochromia, but it's rare. Just like he is rare…to me, at least. I have never seen a guy that is so beautiful. I watch his eyes sweep the room, captivating in his wake. You just can't help but notice him when he enters a room.

Jess turns around when she notices me staring at the five guys and two girls heading to the bar. I try to act like I'm watching them as a group, but in all honesty, there is only one

I have eyes for. He is tall, chiseled with muscle under his black long-sleeve sweater and dark jeans.

I motion with my hand to the hot-ass guy that did me a solid by pointing me in the right direction to find the building I was looking for. "Who is he?"

Jess laughs through her nose and shakes her head. "That is Dravin Beckford, also a senior." She turns to look at me and snaps her fingers to get my attention before lowering her voice. "Stay away from him. He is one of the richest guys that attend here and a total player. He's a fuck 'em and leave 'em type of guy. The girl with white porcelain skin and straight black hair, her name is Veronica and she's a total bitch. Stay away from her. The other one with red hair is Lizzy, and she follows Veronica in everything that she does, including screwing people over. The seven of them are part of the rich, elite Kenyan crew. They can basically do what they want, when they want, and to whoever they want and get away with it."

"What do you mean?"

Her lips form a thin line. When I raise my brow, waiting for her to spill, she sighs, licks her lips, and continues. "The other four guys are just as hot but not as evil as Dravin and his two close friends. You need to watch out for Dravin, Reid, Valen, and Veronica. Veronica is like Dravin in many ways. They aren't together as a couple. They just like to compete."

"Compete? For what?"

"Who they can fuck over first. Who they can destroy for fun because they like to play mindfuck games. Based on what I have seen from my time here, word of advice: stay away from them. They are not like us. They are rich and get away with shit. Especially Veronica."

"Are you sure they aren't together?"

"Who? Dravin and Veronica?"

I nod, curious about them.

"Not that I know of. Maybe in secret. They both do the same things, except Dravin doesn't care what anyone thinks of him. Veronica cares, and she has everyone fooled. She acts like she is Mother Theresa or something, but people know the truth. They're just scared to admit it. She is a liar and, from what I have heard, a total slut but in front of everyone, she acts like a saint. So, she could be hiding things."

"They look very cozy to me," I say, nudging my head toward the group as they play pool on the other side of the bar. Dravin and Veronica are standing close together, whispering something to each other.

"I'm almost positive they aren't together. She was dating this guy named Warren."

"Who's Warren?" I ask, intrigued.

"Warren is rich and popular and an athlete. The five guys you saw enter the bar are all on the swim team. Swimming here is a big deal; the other guys they are playing pool with are also on the team. Warren was going out with Veronica until they parted ways last semester. She claims they were just giving each other a break, but according to him, he dumped her. Let's just say she didn't take it very well because it dented her ego."

"Why do you think he dumped her?"

She shrugs. "No one knows, but it seems she isn't over him. She still hangs around the guys on the swim team and since Dravin is the captain, she figures that if she stays tight with him and the others, Warren will show up and things will return to the way they were."

"Obviously, it isn't working."

"Nope. I think he is over her or just simply sick of her shit. The way she acts behind the scenes, you would think she is the devil's daughter and Dravin is the devil's son. I'm surprised the church attached to the school doesn't go up in flames when they enter for Sunday mass. Promise me you will stay away from them."

"I'm not interested in any of their games."

"Oh, and one more thing... Don't fuck any of the rich guys. They are all players and will tell you what you want to hear to get in your pants. I've watched many girls get destroyed by these guys. Don't say I didn't warn you."

I take a sip of my drink and when I place my cup down, eyes from across the pool table meet mine. They should be aimed at the ball for the winning shot, but they aren't. The light hanging over the pool table casts a glow over his face. One dark eye, one light eye, watching me like I'm the intended target. It's like Dravin wants to see inside my head. He wants to know what I'm thinking. What makes me tick.

The sound of the tip of the pool stick meeting the ball as he slides his fingers over the stick snaps me out of the trance he had me in. Averting my gaze, it lands on Jess.

"Stay away," she whispers. "He is controlling, and he loves a challenge. Once he is bored with you, he will humiliate you just for participating."

"Sounds like a standup guy. Who should I pay attention to then?"

She gives me a smirk. "Normal people who earn the things they are given and have morals. Translation, almost no one. There are a handful of scholarship students and the ones that have to pay their way through college. Some of them get corrupted and sucked in like little pets of the elite, but you will figure it out. I have faith in you. You don't seem like the type to fall into temptation," she says, giving me a wink.

I down the rest of my drink, but the watered-down mixture of cranberry and vodka is not as strong when it hits my stomach. I give her a smirk and say, "Like Dravin?"

"Yes," she answers.

My bladder decides to announce that it needs to be emptied, or I'll be swimming in the next five minutes. It will also give me time to wrap my mind around what Jess told me about Dravin and his crew of friends.

"I'm going to the bathroom, and then we can head back," I tell her.

"Alright. I'll finish my drink by the time you get back."

———

When I slide my pants up, the toilet automatically flushes, and I head to the sink to wash my hands. I watch as the water rinses the soap off my hands, swirling into the drain, forming little bubbles. When I turn to grab a paper towel, I'm suddenly aware that I'm not alone in the bathroom. My head turns to the left and I jolt biting back a scream.

"You scared me," I blurt.

My stomach begins to twist and buzz, and my heart begins to beat wildly inside my chest like I'm having a panic attack. Leaning against the wall in the dark, casting shadows on the dimly lit bathroom, is Dravin. His eyes sweep down my skinny jeans, his exotic eyes studying me like I'm an exhibit in a zoo.

When I find my voice, I quirk a brow. "Can I help you?"

His eyes slowly travel up until it reaches my face. "I've never seen you before. What year are you?"

"You saw me yesterday, and you pointed me toward my dorm. I'm a senior. I transferred in from Wisconsin."

"I didn't ask all that. Now tell me, do you have a boyfriend?"

"No. Do you?"

He chuckles, and my heart speeds up when I see how breathtaking he looks when he laughs. The sound coming from his beautiful face, with eyes that look like they have seen centuries of existence, makes me forget that I'm alone in the women's bathroom in a bar called the Babylon with the most intriguing man I've ever been around.

"No. Are you a lesbian?"

My brows raise in annoyance. "No," I quip, turning around to toss the brown paper towel into the waste basket.

"Nice."

When I turn back around, I sigh, disgusted. "Are you always this charming when you meet women?

"You have a nice ass. I was just pointing it out."

He moves close and I take a step back, my lower back hitting the edge of the counter. "Do you always stalk women when they go to the bathroom to check out their ass?"

"Don't get ahead of yourself. I was just coming in here to do you a favor and tell you not to listen to everything you hear. I don't appreciate people spreading rumors about me."

"What are you talking about?

My chin raises, and his gaze falls to my throat like a vampire wanting a taste of blood. His lips are inches from the side of my neck. I can smell his cologne, expensive, but refined. The type of scent that gets addicting when you first inhale. Dravin is like a drug wrapped in a blanket of temptation.

My mother would tell me that when you are trapped in temptation, you can either hop on it and ride it, or kneel, and pray it goes away. Now I understand what she meant.

His exotic eyes find mine, and I don't know which one is salvation or damnation. It is like looking into a lens of good versus evil—terrifyingly beautiful.

"Most people are morons. Don't believe everything you hear and don't knock what you haven't tried."

"I wasn't interested in trying anything."

His lips skim the skin on my neck, and it feels like lightning strikes before an impending storm, instantly making me a liar. His lips reach the lobe of my ear and the tiny hairs on my skin lift. Oh, fuck. I don't breathe. I don't move.

"Liar," he whispers.

The breath I was holding leaks from my lips. My head turns, and my lips are inches from the stubble of his cheek. He smells of bourbon, cologne, and me. His eyes feast on the exposed skin of my shoulder like he can read my thoughts. The only way I can take back control is if I deny him.

"Just because girls fall at your feet, and let you sleep with them, doesn't mean I'm one of them."

Silence stretches for a few seconds before he asks, "How do you know I sleep with them?"

I lie. "A friend texted me."

His jaw ticks, indicating I struck a nerve. "Maybe you should get to know a person before you make those types of assumptions and judge them based on gossip."

I feel like an ass and the last thing I need is to piss people like Dravin off. Who am I to judge?

"I'm sorry. I shouldn't have said that, but you can't expect me not to react when you get close to me just because you think I want you."

"Do you?"

My head tilts back to look at him. This close, I notice Dravin is way taller than me, and I'm five-foot-six. I already apologized, and he is being dramatic, but I won't throw Jess under the bus. I don't need problems with my roommate. I have only been here forty-eight hours, and the last thing I need is problems with rich people who can make my life miserable. He's probably trying to figure out if he can mess with me or mess with my head.

"Look, I said I was sorry. Let's start over. My name is Gia." I stick my hand out between us and he steps back. He stays quiet for a second. A second turns into a few more. He is probably not used to a girl acting normal and not bending over in his presence hoping he will have mercy and screw them. His hand slides into mine, and we shake.

"I'm Dravin."

I give him my best smile, but before he releases my hand, his thumb makes circular motions in the palm of my hand. My nipples harden under the cups of my bra, and I feel my mouth part. I have never felt this aroused by a guy before, but I'm quickly learning how to keep myself in check. If there are more guys like Dravin who attend here, then I'm really going to have to work on my body language and keep my thoughts to myself as much as possible.

His voice lowers into a husky tone. "Tell me, Gia. I'm curious. You are obviously not the type that would allow me to turn you around and pull those jeans over that sexy ass and take you right here from behind. Do you play with yourself?"

I glare at him, snatching my hand back. I go around him and storm out of the bathroom. Fucking asshole. This is all a game to him. He wants to see if I'll let him fuck me in a restroom of a bar, if I'm the type to give in. Like I would tell him something like that.

"It was just a question to get to know you better," he mocks as I stomp through the hallway back to the table where Jess is waiting to leave.

CHAPTER THREE

GIA

JESS ASKED last night if I was ok because, according to her, I came out of the bathroom flushed. More like pissed the fuck off and aroused all at the same time. The guy is totally full of himself and a total dick. What the fuck was that? I didn't tell her what happened with Dravin in the bathroom because nothing happened except that she was right: he is a player, and I need to stay away from him.

"Hi." A guy's voice says from behind me in class.

Turning around, I find a brown-haired, green-eyed Adonis staring at me with a smile on his face. I was right. All the guys around here look lethal.

Peering around, I notice he was talking to me.

"Hi," he repeats. "My name is Warren, and you are?"

Alarm bells begin to go off—more like the sound of a foghorn going off in my head, warning me not to make conversation with this guy. Jess warned me about Dravin, and look how that turned out. That means this guy is definitely in a no-fly zone. I don't need the wrath of the devil's daughter, Veronica. I just need to complete this year and graduate, and I will never have to see these people again.

Giving him a stern look, I answer. "Gia."

"Gia," he repeats. "I like it. It reminds me of Gia, the supermodel."

His attempt at flattery amuses me. He didn't say I looked like her, but because of my name, it reminded him of her. She was a beautiful model who was dealing with her demons and lived a tragic life.

"You know she was a heroin addict and died of AIDS-related complications. She turned to drugs to battle the dark side of modeling and to deal with childhood issues and relationships. It is a tragic story. I'm glad I remind you of her."

His mouth drops, leaving him with a confused expression, and I turn around. It was the only response I could think of that would make him feel uncomfortable, so he wouldn't continue talking to me.

The professor hands me the syllabus, and when I stretch my arm to pass back the stack of papers, Warren takes them but places a small piece of paper in my hand.

I take it and look down to read it.

I didn't mean to offend you. How about I apologize with a cup of coffee? 216-433-7898
Warren

The professor looks directly at me, and I have no choice but to slip the paper into my bag.

The professor looks young for his age, or he ages well. He appears no more than in his late thirties or early forties, wearing a dress shirt and slacks. His hair is styled with gel, and he wears glasses. His eyes zero in on me and my leg begins to bounce under my desk.

"I see we have a new student this year. Would you please introduce yourself to the class? Most of your peers are in the same economics major and will be graduating alongside you. You should get to know them better."

The professor gives Warren and me a knowing look, but I

dismiss it, figuring that he saw him hand me the small piece of paper. It doesn't take a genius to know Warren was flirting with me or trying to ask me out.

I introduce myself to the class and tell them I transferred in from Wisconsin and what I'm majoring in.

After class, I walk outside the building and pull up the campus map on my phone, looking for the cafeteria to grab some lunch. I was able to get a meal plan and based on what I have heard from Jess, I'm sure the cafeteria is empty. The rich don't eat in the cafeteria. They eat at local restaurants and cafés every day.

"Hey." I hear Warren's voice call out.

I stop and turn around, and he stops right in front of me. "How about that coffee?"

Shaking my head. "You don't give up, do you?"

"Not when I'm interested in something."

"Well, thank goodness I'm not a thing." I deadpan and turn away. "Good luck, I hope it works out."

He follows quickly alongside me. "Are you always this difficult when a guy shows an interest in getting to know you?"

"No, I just didn't come to this school for the sole purpose of hooking up. I don't know you, and you don't know me."

"That is what the coffee invite is for—to get to know you."

"Don't you have a girlfriend or something?"

He shakes his head, his playful demeanor diminishing when I mention the girlfriend question.

"No. I don't have a girlfriend. Not anymore. I dumped her before last semester ended; she was a psychotic, sex-crazed, head case."

"Wow. I would have thought a girl into crazy sex would be a good thing."

"Not like that. She is on a whole other level than what I'm down with."

He keeps walking beside me, and to be honest, I still have no idea where I'm going, but he keeps following me anyway. I'm intrigued by the way he talks about the girl he broke up with. I know it's Veronica, but he doesn't give away her name. Interesting. He doesn't know I know who he is referring to since I'm new here, so I test him.

"That must have sucked. Who was she?"

"I'd rather keep that to myself. It doesn't matter; we weren't exclusive. It's over." He looks around nervously, and then his gaze lands back on mine. "Do you know where you are going?"

He doesn't want to put her out there. I guess what Jess said is true. He is afraid of Veronica's wrath. I don't want to seem rude, but then Dravin's comment about gossip and thinking the worst about people because of rumors pops into my head. He wasn't creepy or anything, and he didn't corner me in the women's restroom to seduce me.

I sigh and give him a grin. "Honestly, I was trying to see if you would get tired and give up following me, but to answer your question. I'm looking for the cafeteria to grab lunch."

His eyes rake over my simple black shirt, jeans, and docs. "How about I take you?"

My brow lifts. "Where?"

"To lunch. I want to take you out to lunch. It will be my treat."

"I don't think that is a good idea."

"Why not? There is no reason why we couldn't go to lunch as friends."

He seems harmless and it's not like I will let it get any further than eating lunch at the same place. He just happened to be there. Maybe he will give me more information on Dravin and the people he hangs around with.

For some reason, Dravin intrigues me. He comes off as an ass, but nonetheless, he has this air of confidence about him, like he doesn't care what people think. Except in the bathroom, he cared what Jess was telling me about him. Dravin cared what I thought about him and that is what got my attention. Why?

How would he know she would talk bad about him is a mystery. It bothered him that I saw him as a guy with a bad rep. Why would he care? He made it seem that it was all a test to see if I was down to have a quickie in the bathroom. Dravin looks dangerous compared to Warren. Warren seems harmless and he doesn't talk to me like Dravin does. He isn't forward with the sexual innuendos that make me drip between my thighs, imagining what color his eyes turn when he has sex. Would they stay the same, or would they darken and change colors?

"Alright, but as friends."

His lips lift in a smile. "I promise I will behave. We can go to the café two blocks away. We could walk, or would you rather we drive there?"

My lip is snagged by my bottom teeth as I ponder if we should walk or drive. I don't have a car, and that means I would have to let him drive me. I don't know him, so I go with the safer route.

"I don't have a car." My cheeks heat in embarrassment and I look behind him.

He walks closer, his book bag slung over one shoulder, and he slides his light brown hair away from his eyes. He is tall but a tad shorter than Dravin. His forearms are corded with muscle, but not like Dravin's, and I look away, mentally kicking myself for comparing Warren to Dravin. *What in the hell is wrong with me?*

Since meeting Dravin, I have been comparing all the guys that are attractive to him. He is every definition of a bad boy and has the mouth to go with it. But those eyes. His eyes are the most mysterious quality about him, both light and dark. I can't seem to stop myself from thinking about them.

Warren lowers his voice a fraction, "If you feel better walking, Gia, I'm cool with it. I understand if you don't feel comfortable having me drive you."

Feeling relieved, my shoulders sag and I let out a small breath I was holding. "Okay. I appreciate that. A walk it is, then."

"What time is your next class?" He asks, turning in the direction of the café, which is, in fact, in the opposite direction.

"In an hour and a half."

"Good, my class doesn't start until two hours from now. We have enough time to head over and back without either of us missing class."

He walks beside me. Close but not too far. He keeps a friendly distance, but I still feel guarded and on edge. He seems nice. Remembering what Jess told me and from my encounter with Dravin, I know I still have to be careful in this place. I will have to keep everyone I encounter at a safe distance.

CHAPTER FOUR

DRAVIN

THERE IS a knock on my bedroom door. "What?" I shout back.

The knob of my door turns, and Reid, my roommate, appears in the doorway. I click the mouse and close all the windows on the screens I had open. Turning toward him, I glare at Reid.

"My bad, brother, I was letting you know you have a visitor."

"I could have knocked, and I'm not just any visitor. I have a name," Veronica says, practically pushing Reid aside so she can walk inside my bedroom.

Reid rolls his eyes. He hates Veronica because he knows what she is capable of. She's almost the female version of me and rumor has it, I'm most likely the son of Lucifer himself. The main difference between Veronica and I is that I have a terrible rep and have no fucks to give compared to Veronica. She has everyone except the people she has fucked over convinced she's Marsha fucking Brady.

"To what do I owe the pleasure?" I mock.

She gives me a devious smile. Which can only mean one thing, she wants to fuck or destroy someone.

She licks her lips seductively and turns her head, speaking to Reid. "Leave us," she demands.

He gives her the finger and she makes a silent motion with her hand in a fist like she is sucking a dick. "In your dreams. It will never happen. I don't fuck losers."

Reid gives her a disgusted expression. "Don't worry, I'm not interested in fucking demons."

He shuts the door with a click.

Leaning back in my gaming chair, my gaze lands on Veronica. "What do you want?"

"I need a favor."

"Whatever it is, hell no."

Veronica's favors are dangerous and risky. It will always involve fucking over someone I have no interest in fucking over, and let's face it, it's dull. Chicks and their drama don't do it for me, and Veronica is full of drama. If she doesn't get her way, she pouts and throws a tantrum like a three-year-old.

The only reason she is even allowed in my house is because we have known her since high school. Our fathers know each other and have done business together. You would think they would want to play matchmaker, but the problem with that scenario is her gold-digging mother was caught fucking my father after my mother committed suicide. Her father didn't divorce her, of course, but he started fucking whoever he wanted, even in their bed, if he wanted.

Her mother was forbidden from continuing the affair, but my father and Veronica's father continued to be friends and colleagues. It wasn't my father's fault Veronica's mother is a gold-digging whore. His words, not mine.

"I need your help, Dravin," she purrs.

Her skirt is shorter than it should be, with her fake breasts pushed together in her skimpy blouse and heels. One thing Veronica and I have never done, is fuck. I would fuck her, but she loves to try and play games. She knows I'm the puppet master. There is no game she can win with me, and she knows it. I am always in control. I need, and I crave it.

Not even my father can control me. After my mother slit her wrists and drowned in a bathtub full of water, something changed in me. I can't give control to anyone, not even God. Since my mother died, God and I have had a rocky relationship.

"Why should I help you? Not that I give a fuck what you want. There is nothing you could offer me that I want."

She walks close to me. My legs are slightly apart, and I'm facing her as she steps closer. Her hand slides up her thigh, disappearing under her short skirt, lifting it to flash me her completely see-through panties. I tilt my head to take a look at what she is offering.

Her two fingers slide beside her lower lips squishing them together.

"I'll give you something you've never had."

My dick twitches because she is touching something I've never had from her. Some people think we fuck on the down low, but that is not the truth. Not that I wouldn't mind sliding my cock inside her and giving her a ride.

She removes her hand and straddles me. She rubs herself on the crotch of my long basketball shorts and I'm rocking a semi. Veronica is a beautiful woman with a tiny waist and blonde wavy hair, but her soul is dark and evil. She isn't my type, except a fuck is still just that, a fuck.

I'm as dark and corrupted as it is, but throwing her into the mix is like the devil's children having an orgy. Not my thing.

"Come on, Dravin, do this for me? Pleeese," she coos.

She places her hands on my shoulders to whisper in my ear and continues to rub her pussy on the tip of my cock over my shorts. She is doing what she does best behind closed doors. She seduces to get what she wants.

"I'll let you stick it anywhere," she whispers. "Any-where," she repeats.

My nostrils flare. Her lips graze my cheek, and my dick goes rock hard. I'm a man, and a beautiful woman is strad-dling me and rubbing her pussy on my dick, telling me if I do want she wants, I can fuck her any way I like. But...I push her off me, and she slides off my lap, adjusting her skirt. Like I said, I crave control.

"What do you want?" I ask.

She sits on the bed with her legs open so I can get a good view of what she is offering. "I want you to do some-thing for me. I have a problem," she says in a clipped voice.

Glancing at her pussy, I motion for her to get up and open her legs wider while she stands. She does, and I lean back on my chair and look up at her face with a stern expression, showing her that it will take a lot more convincing. I don't like to fuck girls on my bed. I dismiss them when I'm done; the last thing I want is their smell on my sheets. If she is mad I told her to get up off my bed, she doesn't say anything. Whatever she wants me to do, it must be very important to her.

"What problem? Does Warren have a small dick, and you need me to remind you what a big dick can do?"

"Ha-ha... very funny," she parrots.

"Didn't you two part ways last semester?" I ask.

"We're taking a break."

I sneer and raise a brow.

She places her hands on her hips and huffs. "Okay, he dumped me."

I motion for her to open her legs wider. This is interesting and I like to mess with her. She thinks she will get whatever she wants from me, but come to think of it, I'm bored. I want to know what she wants me to do.

I'm bored with fucking stupid college girls who get clingy and stalkerish. They think that if they give it up, and you have sex, it is a sign of commitment. It's hard to find one that just wants to fuck, and I hardly have any time to go outside off campus to wine and dine with a woman just to have sex. If I do fuck outside off campus, it's to destroy a person. Sure, I get pleasure from getting my dick wet, but I get more pleasure by destroying the person the act was intended to hurt.

She widens her stance, and I smirk, loving the control I'm having over her.

"What's wrong? You didn't swallow."

"Fuck you, Dravin."

"That's what you're offering me. Your words, not mine. Now what the fuck do you want? And you better make it fast. I'm losing my patience, and you're about to get asked to leave."

"Fine. Warren said we could be friends after he dumped me, but lately, he has been ghosting me and is all up this new girl's ass. I passed by the café, and he was having lunch with her. She is pretty with dark hair, full breasts, and full of… virtue. You can tell she is innocent. Her body language is sexy and hot but also…unintended."

"Who is this girl? Just ruin her like you do everyone that gets in your way."

"It is not that easy because Warren really likes her. It would be obvious if I did anything. It's too soon for me to bare my teeth. He looks at her the way he used to look at me, and I know he wants her." She arches her back and looks up, straightening and staring directly at me. "He wants to fuck her. Her name is Gia or something."

My eyes snap to hers when I hear that name rolling off her

tongue—the new girl, the one I followed into the restroom at Babylon.

The one that I wanted to bend over to hear her scream my name while I gave her an orgasm we both would remember. The one that denied me. She's the type I can't use my charms on because someone has already poisoned her mind about me. They have told her the truth, whereas I told her a lie that wasn't true. She believed them, and not me, and I was irked. The way her jeans molded the curves of her ass and her straight hair and black manicured nails. *Gia*. Her name on my lips does something to me. I want her. I want to see the expression her face makes when I make her come. I want to taste every drop of her lust until she sees me as her God.

The image of her I play in my mind wearing a black negligée and red bottom heels while she worships my cock after fucking every hole in her body is imprinted in my mind. It's what I think about when I jerked off before I went to bed, when I fucked the blonde after class, and this morning when I jerked off in the shower.

"What about her?" I ask, keeping a straight face.

"I want you to seduce her. I want you to fuck her and then humiliate her by leaving her publicly. If Warren knows you fucked her, he will forget about her. He can't stand you, and he would never pursue her if he found out she rode your cock."

"What happens when you ride mine?"

"He won't find out because we won't tell him. I get his attention, and you get what you have been dying to have for years, and that is for you to fuck your brains out in every hole that big cock of yours can fit in." She slides her panties to the side so I can get a better view of her cunt by lifting her skirt. "You want this?" She twirls her fingers over her clit, and I sit up and watch the show.

"Maybe."

She stands between my legs with her legs open. My eyes find hers. "So, what is going to be? It's a win-win for you. You get her pussy, and then you get mine. You don't lose." My hand slides up and I cup her pussy as I stand. She gasps as she takes a step back. "You're soaked," I tell her, my voice laced with steel inches from her lips. "I love the way you have to blackmail me to fuck me." I slide a finger over her clit, and she whimpers.

She places her hands on my muscled chest. "Dravin?"

"Yeah."

Her head tilts up to look at me, and she says, "I'm soaked because I'm imagining you fucking her."

I snatch my hand back and wipe her arousal on her blouse. "Liar. Get out," I demand in a rigid tone.

She swallows, embarrassed that I dismissed her like the whore she is, but I respect her control, just like her father. Her mother doesn't have any. In truth, Veronica has a shitty father and mother. They both expect her to be posh and perfect in the eyes of society, yet they're not.

Like my father, they sent her from the elite society of Ohio to Kenyan University to be closer to the church and accept God. Funny, they don't live by God's rules, although they expect us to follow rules that they didn't.

She opens the door of my house located on the exclusive street the campus students call Millionaire's Row. She turns around before she crosses the threshold, "Will you?"

"Fine. I'll do it."

Her lips lift like Cruella Deville from the Dalmatians. "If you can't do it, I'll ruin her another way, and the deal is off."

"I'll win. I always win."

"Good, I was starting to get worried."

"Why is that?"

"I could tell you were getting bored lately. Next thing you know, you will be fucking the nuns that come to the church from the convent to help out."

"Not my style," I quip.

She turns and walks out. "Yeah, right."

If she only knew, I'd already had my eye on Gia, but now Veronica has let me know, and so does everyone else. And that is a problem.

CHAPTER FIVE

GIA

"EVERYONE IS TALKING about you and Warren the other day," Jess says.

My brows pinch and I place my laptop down on the bed and sit up on the twin bed in our dorm. "Everyone?"

She fixes the strap of her tank top, adjusts her breasts in her bra, and quirks her brow. "Everyone. Including Warren."

What the hell. It was just lunch. Why would he make it out more than it was? *Because he is a rich prick and Jess warned you, but you didn't listen.*

"It was lunch, and I only allowed it because he felt awkward about telling me that my name reminded him of the supermodel who died."

"The poor young woman that was hooked on heroin? The girl died of AIDS. She was gorgeous but tragic all at the same time."

"That's the one."

She snorts. "What an idiot. He really doesn't have game."

I wave my hand. "Exactly. I pointed that out to him. He realized how bad it sounded and I was trying to be nice by accepting his offer to go to lunch. It was harmless, and I didn't intend for it to look like anything other than what it was. Lunch."

She curls her legs so she sits crisscrossed on her bed. "It obviously meant more to him and everyone else who happened to be there or pass by. You better hope that Veronica is over him and on to someone else."

Great, that means I'll be public enemy number one if I'm not already.

"I'm her target now, aren't I?"

She bites her lip and scrunches her nose, the seconds ticking by as I wait silently. My anxiety is already climbing to atomic levels. She inhales, her chest inflates, and lets out an audible breath. "You're fucked bitch. No one has said anything yet. It has only been four days, and today is Friday. Let's get the fuck out of here and go to Babylon. We'll hang out, have a couple of drinks, get fucked up, and laugh. Hopefully, you can find a hot guy, smash, which means fuck by the way. The shit about Warren will be a distant memory. Word will get around that you hooked up with someone else, and all will be good."

I lay back on my firm pillow, cursing that I don't have enough money to buy the downier one I want. Hating how I got myself into this situation after Jess clearly warned me about it. My naïve ass fell for it. But it doesn't mean that I have to screw someone just to get out of it.

"Fine, but I'm not sleeping with anyone."

She snickers, placing her hand over her mouth. "Why? You're not a virgin, are you?"

My head turns, and I gaze at her and then look up, not telling her the truth, hoping she will just drop it. Getting up, I shut down my computer and put my economics assignment away.

She gets up to begin finding something to wear. "You are, aren't you? That is why you are freaking out and are not interested in hooking up."

I slam the drawer shut, annoyed that she figured me out. "So what if I am? I just haven't found the right person to get it over with, and back where I'm from, my parents were this church-going perfect couple who had it all figured out until they divorced. It was all a bunch of bullshit packed with lies. They never let me date, gave me shit about liking boys. I figured that I would just fuck some guy and get it over with and live my life like a normal teenager. Now I'm twenty-one and still haven't done it because I just got away from their drama by coming here."

"Relax, boo. It's not that big of a deal." She grimaces her face in pity. "I take that back. Here, it is that big of a deal, especially with guys like Dravin lurking around in all his deliciousness. That guy will eat you alive. You'll probably love it, though."

"Love what?" I snap.

Her mentioning Dravin is rubbing me the wrong way. The guy is scorching hot, no doubt about that. He has this gothic bad-boy vibe I have never encountered before. The type you see or hear about in movies. His eyes are like a deadly sin waiting to devour you. *More like what's between my legs.* The thought makes me wet, and a thumping feeling pulsates from my clit. Instead of my heart beating widely, it's my clit thumping wildly, wanting God knows what. But the devil knows...Dravin knows. I have to shamefully admit that my last encounter had me playing with myself in the shower and I came twice. On my own. Thinking of...him.

"Letting Dravin Bedford fuck you and pop that cherry. Damn girl, I can't even imagine it. I haven't experienced it myself, but from what I have heard, the man has a huge dick."

"He probably paid some girl to say that or threatened her. But I thought he was off limits, and I should stay away?"

She shakes her head. "I've changed my mind. Every girl walks funny after a night with Dravin. They don't complain about it all. They just want more, but he's a one-time rip-and-dip kind of guy. I know I told you to stay away, but you need to fuck someone who is a one-time type of guy."

I giggle. "Rip and dip? Really?"

She cackles. "Yeah, he is only with a girl once and never repeats or fucks the same chick twice." She waves her hand. "And, I have heard he never goes down on a girl. No one, I mean no one, has ever said the boy eats pussy." She shrugs. "Figured he doesn't for whatever reason."

I hold up an outfit in each hand. "Enough about goth boy. Which one?"

She points to the one on the left with the fishnets, short skirt, and grunge tee. "That one. A goth boy will dig the fishnets."

"I'm not going there to impress the poster boy for Hot Topic."

She laughs. "Oh, man. I am totally going to tell him you said that."

I laugh with her, not caring if she does or doesn't. I still haven't told her about my encounter with Dravin, and I don't plan on telling her because it doesn't matter. Dravin is a fuckboy and I'm not into fuckboys.

———

We are seated in the same booth as last week, but this time, there isn't a hot bad boy playing pool with a stick watching me from across the room. "Greedy Fly" by Bush plays from the bar's jukebox, giving the place a 90s alternative rock vibe.

"I like this song," I tell Jess, nursing a vodka and cranberry.

"Me too. Is that all you ever drink?" She points to my cup.

"It's what I can handle."

A voice not belonging to Jess answers. "Not much, apparently."

Blonde locks frame a white porcelain face with painted, maroon-colored lips and tight leather pants under a white cropped top.

"To what do we owe the pleasure, Veronica?" Jess asks with a scowl.

"Oh Jess, are you still mad about that little thing from last year," she purrs.

I glance from Jess to Veronica, wondering what Veronica was talking about. "What little thing from last year?"

Jess' eyes flash with pure anger, but Veronica looks— amused. Jess glances at me, and she must notice that I'm giving Veronica my resting bitch face. Whatever went on, is not my problem. For the past week, Jess has been friendly to me and everything she has said about the people who attend Kenyan has been true. So far.

Veronica smiles at me and then leans close. She may be beautiful, but her attitude spoils it. I can't even blame Warren. Sleeping with this bitch must have been like lying in a bed of snakes. They can all bite you. You just don't know when, and it's best to crawl out while you can.

Veronica glances at me like I'm a meal, and I lean back, my upper lip curling in a snarl. "She's very pretty, Jess. I like her dark hair and just look at those lips." She lowers her voice and whispers loud enough over the music. "Ripe for sucking."

"Fuck off," I sneer.

She licks her lips seductively and backs away. The bar's front door opens, and it's already dark outside. Warren comes inside, followed by the rest of the swim team, including Dravin.

The air in the entire place changes, and that catches the

evil bitch's attention. She skitters off in their direction. It is like a group of celebrities walking inside the building. All conversation seizes. You can tell because the music coming from the jukebox seems to have gotten louder.

After watching Veronica saunter toward the group of guys, my head whips toward Jess. "She's disgusting. If you don't mind me asking, what happened?" I down the rest of my drink and place the glass on the table with a clunk.

Jess swallows and takes a big gulp of her drink. "She saw I was interested in a guy, and she convinced him to have sex with me out of pity. We went on two dates, and then he agreed, but he wanted me with another girl at the same time. I liked him, and she knew that, but it didn't stop her from playing mind games. She manipulates people into getting what she wants. She feeds off it. That's why you need to stay away from Warren."

"Did you?"

"Did I what?"

"Do it?"

She takes another long gulp until she drains the glass and places it down on the table. "Yeah, I did."

"Holy shit," I mutter.

"Then he said he couldn't go out with me because I did and that he did it out of pity going on and on about some bull-shit Veronica fed him about me wanting to explore my sexuality."

"What a fucking asshole."

She snorts. "I know. She fucked him right after, and he liked it a little too much. She had to threaten to publicly humiliate him if he didn't stop coming after her."

"Who is this asshole?"

"Garret. Third dick on the right talking to Dravin."

"So, everyone on the swim team is a conceited fuckboy. Got it."

She snickers. "I love that about you. You don't care and catch on quickly."

I shake my head. "Honestly, we all have stories, and we all want things. It is up to us to give or take with care. Everyone needs to rebalance at some point. If something goes bad or is not the way you envisioned it, change it and learn from it."

Jess nods. She points to my drink. "Another?"

"Yeah, something I can definitely handle so I can stay alert and watch out for crazy bitches with a complex. How about you?"

Jess throws her head back and laughs. "No, I'm good. I like you, Gia. You have a great sense of humor. Be careful with Veronica, though. She has claws, and they hurt."

"I see that. All I have heard about her are good things," I say jokingly.

The bartender puts a round of drinks on the bar and the rest of the swim team along with Veronica head out to the billiard tables. Veronica watches Warren like a hawk while she chats up Dravin like they are old friends who haven't seen each other and are catching up. It wouldn't surprise me if they were intimate. They look like they would be good together. Physically, at least. Veronica may come off as a psycho bitch when you meet her, but you cannot deny that she is beautiful. They probably should sleep together with their winning personalities.

"What can I get you?" the male bartender asks, slinging a little white towel over his shoulder while he leans on the edge of the bar.

My head turns, and the blonde, blue-eyed, young

bartender smirks at me when he catches where my attention was a few moments ago.

He nudges his head toward the pool tables. "Kenyan's finest. You know them?"

I shake my head. "I would like a vodka and cranberry, please?"

"Coming right up."

My head tilts and I find Jess seated at the booth, her stare locked over at the pool tables like she is looking for someone and hasn't found them yet. She must feel me staring right at her because her eyes land on mine, and I quirk a brow, silently asking her—*Who are you looking for?*

The bartender returns with my mixed drink and slides it behind me on the bar top. When I turn my body back to the bartender to hand him my card, his gaze lands behind me, but I notice a hint of fear on his face before it quickly disappears.

"Put it on my tab. Whatever she wants."

My eyes close as Dravin's dry, stern tone filters through my skin, prickling in awareness. Electricity courses through me as he stands behind me without uttering another word. The bartender glances at me with my card in his hand.

"Charge my card, please," I counter, my eyes not wavering.

The bartender looks nervous, unsure of what to do, but one more glance at Dravin has my hopes go up in smoke. The bartender shakes his head and hands me back my card.

He gives me a smirk, but I know he is just trying to play it off because that same flash of fear I witnessed a moment ago crosses his expression. "I'm sorry, but if a guy wants to buy a girl a drink and she clearly knows him, I'm gonna have to allow it. Bar rules."

"What? Are you kidding me?" I hiss. "I don't know him."
I point my thumb behind me.

His lips tip upward in a grin. "Yes, you do. It's okay."

"You heard me. Don't listen to her. Give her back the card
and charge whatever drinks she has had on my tab."

Anger begins to spike through me. I turn around to find
two different color eyes boring into me, a fitted Henley, and
black jeans sitting low on his hips. This time, he has a thin
ring pierced in his nose adding to his sex appeal. His jaw is
clenched, and a muscle tics on the left side of his jaw.

His full lips look perfect, and I ache to know how they
would feel on mine. Memories from our last encounter in the
bathroom replay like a rerun. His scent when he was up close
and the way he looked at me full of pure lust awakened a need
inside me I didn't realize I possessed. His tongue peeks out,
and his upper lip curls in a sexy grin, and I'm still imagining
how his lips would feel against mine. Would they feel soft,
hard, or smooth? His head is positioned straight ahead, but his
eyes move downward without tilting his neck to watch me.

Breaking the tension between us, I ask, "Why did you
insist on paying for my drinks? Do you expect me to sleep
with you now?"

He chuckles, and it grates on my nerves. The guy is hot,
but he gets under my skin when he mocks me.

"What is so funny?"

He leans close and tilts his head so his lips are close
enough to my ear that I can feel his breath fan against my
skin, making my nipples harden under my bra. I try to fight
the attraction and move away, but when I step back, my back
hits the bar's edge. My head turns, and his lips are inches from
mine, just like last time we were in the bathroom.

"The fact that you want to sleep with me. I bet you

wonder how it would feel for me to slide between your legs. It wouldn't take much, would it?"

My nostrils flare. Anger boiling in my veins. How can a guy be so beautiful and infuriating at the same time?

"You can't help it, can you? Look, I'm not interested in a fuckboy. Keep the drink or give it to some who falls for your shit," I snap, walking around him leaving him alone at the bar with my drink.

I head back over to the booth where Jess is sitting, and I can feel the heat of his stare behind me like a furnace, making my skin flush.

CHAPTER SIX

GIA

"ARE you sure you don't want me to go with you, Gia?" Jess asks with a concerned expression.

After walking away from Dravin and leaving him hanging at the bar, he returns to the pool tables. I grip the handle of my bag and tell Jess I'm leaving. I don't want to go, but I don't trust myself enough around Dravin. The plus side of this situation is that I'm not drunk or even slightly buzzed. I've only had one drink since we got here, but as soon as Dravin got close and riled me up, my brain started telling me to run. Otherwise, I'll end up letting him devour me before the night is over, or worse, he will make me pay for shunning him at the bar.

"I'm good, Jess. It's ok. I know you want to stay."

She has been staring over at the guys on the swim team but has been hesitant because she knows I don't want to hang out over there. Veronica showing up and acting like a creepy psycho bitch is enough to let me know—she doesn't approve of me. She is trying to jerk my chain to see if I rattle, but at this point in my life, I don't think anything can get to me.

Her face falls and a worried line creases her forehead. "I—"

Placing my hand on her shoulder, I give her a warm smile. "It's okay, Jess. Really. I'm going to pee and then I'm going to head back. I'll call you when I make it back to the room. It's all good."

Her shoulders slump in defeat, but her head turns, and she

sighs. "Okay." She leans forward in the booth, placing her hand on the table so she can slide out. "Call me as soon as you make it."

Walking toward the restroom, I wave my hand up not looking back. "I will."

———

I'm leaving the women's restroom when I notice a back door to the bar that reads, "*EXIT.*"

I inwardly sigh, thanking my luck that I won't have to go back out to the front and risk running into Dravin or Veronica. I must admit seeing him so comfortable with her sparks something inside of me that feels a lot like jealousy, but I immediately brush it off.

I'm about to taste victory and exit the bar when the men's restroom door opens. Warren steps out, blocking my path. He reaches out and grips my upper arm to stop me from leaving.

"Hey." I stop and look at his hand and snatch my arm out of his grip. He raises his hands up in surrender. "I didn't mean to grab your arm, but you seemed upset. Is everything alright? I saw Dravin talking to you. Did he say or do anything?"

"Does it matter?"

"If he upset you, I think it does."

I don't feel like talking about it, but I promised myself to be nice and not let people think that they can get to me. "He bought me a drink and I refused."

He raises his brows, shock crossing his features.

"Dravin offered to buy you a drink?"

"Yeah, why is there a problem?"

He shakes his head. "No. Not at all." His brows pinch.

"It's just that he never offers to buy a girl anything, and the fact that you refused says a lot."

"Says a lot about what?

Warren peers down the hall in the other direction like he is hoping he won't get caught by someone. He glances back at me like we are conducting a drug deal or something. What is up with these people? They are sneaky, manipulative, and weird.

"Just…stay away from Dravin. He doesn't have the best reputation."

"Are you warning me off, Dravin?"

He steps closer to me and licks his lips. "Yes, I am."

"Why? Why would you care?"

"Because you seem like a nice girl." He lowers his voice a bit. "And I like you. I know you said the other day at lunch that we were just two people taking the same class, eating at the same place, and nothing more, but… I like you."

Great. This is exactly what I am trying to avoid. The last thing I need is for Warren to be interested in me. Veronica doesn't look like she will take it very well and I don't need issues with psycho chicks who can't take rejection.

Whatever happened between those two, I want no part of it.

"Look, I'm sorry, but I have to get going. You seem very nice, but I'm not interested in any type of relationship right now."

His expression turns serious, and for a second, I think he is going to argue, but then he smiles. Not what I expected. His smile rubs me the wrong way because it feels like it hasn't sunk in that I'm not interested in him. Veronica or no Veronica, Warren is not my type. He seems like a rich snob and I'm a broke college student barely scraping by. We have nothing in common, no chemistry, and he just doesn't make me feel like—*Dravin*. Fuck. I'm comparing already. I really need to get out of here.

"Look, I gotta go. My ride is here."

He steps back and I'm relieved he doesn't follow me out the door.

"I'll see you in class, Gia. I'm glad you were here tonight," he calls out.

Once I'm outside and turn the corner of the building, I'm in the dark. The sidewalk running parallel to the building is desolate and dimly lit. I quickly walk away in case Warren decides to poke his head out and see if I really had a ride. The last thing I need is for him to follow me. The guy acted like I didn't just tell him that I'm in no way interested in him. He brushed it off like we were discussing the weather or what is on next week's study guide.

I'm crossing the street and notice that there is a shortcut through the cemetery behind the church. I have never been superstitious. I'm not scared of the dead. It's the living that one should worry about.

The gates are still open with the lock and chain hanging from the left side. The good news is there are streetlamps along the road leading inside, and I can see that the other side is open and passes by the Catholic church and into the school. It would be more of a risk to walk around on the public sidewalk than taking this route. How many people hang out at the cemetery at night anyway? Calling a cab or the campus rideshare doesn't make sense if all I have to do is cross this way.

I'm passing the tombstones and notice the names. Marie James, 1908, Heath James, 1895. I realize this cemetery is old and has been here for centuries. These people have been buried here for a very long time. Some are family plots full of people with the same last names.

I'm walking and stop when I find the name Bedford on one of them. No way. It can't be. It must be a coincidence.

Anastasia Julianne Bedford, loving wife and mother.
Gone but never forgotten.
April 13, 1981-June 13, 2018.

Looking around, I notice she is the only one in the section alone. I also see that there aren't any flowers here. Most of the graves have flowers, except the really old ones.

I'm not sure if this person is related to Dravin or not, but he isn't the only person in the universe with Bedford as a last name. I'm sure this cemetery has been here way longer than his family has even existed. What are the chances that his family has lived here their whole life? What about his other family members? It seems as if this woman buried here has no other family. Her tombstone is full of dried leaves and spider webs.

I see there is a grave overflowing with flowers. I don't think anyone would mind if I snatched a single red rose to place on her grave. Hastily, I grab a single rose from the grave across and return, placing the red rose on the woman's grave.

I kneel and swipe the area to remove the collected, dried leaves, not caring if my hand gets dirty.

I sigh and decide to at least pay my respects. "I know you don't know me, and I don't know you, but you seemed lonely, and I thought it would be nice for you to have a rose. It seems as if no one has left you any flowers. I hope you don't mind."

"What are you doing?"

I gasp and fall on my butt at the sound of Dravin's deep voice.

I glance up, and he is standing over me with a hard-to-read expression. "What the hell, Dravin?"

He looks at the grave and then back at me as I dust myself off. "What are you doing?" he repeats, his voice stern and almost scary.

"I'm going back to my dorm. What are you the campus stalker? This is the second time you have followed me."

"I wasn't following you."

"Yeah, because people walk through cemeteries at nine o'clock at night all the time after they hang out with friends at a bar." I mock.

He snorts. "Look, just because I offered to fuck you doesn't mean I'm stalking you. Don't flatter yourself."

"Whatever, Goth boy."

"What did you call me?"

I tilt my head up and look at his handsome face. "I said... Whatever, Goth boy."

He points to himself with his thumb to his chest and chuckles. "Goth boy?" He tilts his head up to look at the sky and then his gaze lands on mine when I'm finally standing. "Seriously?"

Waving my hand over his tight body, I motion to his clothes and face. "The different color eyes, always wearing black clothes, the nose piercing. I can go on."

"The nose piercing?"

"Yeah, doesn't help the cause if that's not the look you are going for."

"I like my piercings."

Did he say piercings as in plural, meaning more than one?

"Piercings?"

He nods. "Yeah, I have more than one." He steps closer.

I swallow. "I only see one."

"Do you want to see the other two?

Like an idiot, I respond, "Yeah." I'm curious to see where the others are.

His lips form a smile, and he looks down to the crotch of his pants. He leans in and whispers, "Fuck, you have no idea how bad I want to show you."

My hands cross over my breasts. "Really?" I roll my eyes and turn around, shaking my head. "No thanks. I'm sure I can have someone on campus tell me where they are and what they look like."

"Funny," he blurts sarcastically.

He stands behind me and when I turn my head around, I just stare.

He chuckles. "Are you waiting for me to walk you home?"

My body stiffens, annoyed that he figured me out. I'm also relieved that he didn't say anything about the grave I was kneeling in front of, which means he isn't related to the lady resting there. But then he looks back at it and then looks forward.

When a few seconds pass by, and neither of us moves, he breaks the silence by walking in front of me until he faces me once again. "I'll walk you if you let me kiss you."

I bite my lip in contemplation. If he leaves, I risk walking alone and the fact that he scared me means I'll be even more jumpy, and it probably won't be him startling me the next time.

I shouldn't even be speaking to this guy. I hardly know him, and he has a horrible reputation of being flawed, dangerous, and a heartbreaker. If only he could walk me to my building without any sexual favors, all would be good.

If I take him up on his offer and he chooses to kiss me, I'll have an excuse to actually be kissed by one of the hottest guys I have ever met. Dravin is pure sin wrapped in a delicious body. His offer is dripping with temptation and I don't know if I can resist.

He lifts my chin with his finger, my body stays still, and my eyes remain glued to his handsome face. "Fine. Where?"

He doesn't answer me and walks away but slows down so I can catch up. We walk all the way to the other gate. It is darker on this side of the cemetery, and there is only a single light next to the wrought iron gates. The wind picks up, making the trees groan, and it's at that moment I'm relieved I made the right choice and let Dravin walk with me. The trees continue to sway with the wind like a symphony echoing all around me, blowing my hair away from my face.

He stops and walks to the left toward a secluded pillar where no one can see, even if they pass by. I follow him like I'm in a trance. The peaks of the church seem larger than life, imposing, eerie, and, for some reason, anything but holy.

Goosebumps begin to snake all over my flesh. I know it's not from the cool wind but from the man in front of me. My heart begins to beat in a staccato rhythm in my ear. Dravin is inches from me, and his lips are a breath away. He is so close that we can practically breathe the same air—*slow and even. Inhale, exhale.*

The anticipation of him kissing me is causing the pounding of my heart. The pounding begins to assault my body. It's like the whole world melted away. There is just him and me.

I've been kissed three times in my life, but never by

someone like Dravin. I don't think I have ever met someone as mysterious and interesting as him. His eyes are focused on me, burning like sapphires defying the darkness of the other.

My lips part.

Waiting.

Waiting.

My head tilts up, wanting his lips to touch mine, wanting to experience how they will feel, but his head dips lower, and I inhale when he kisses the side of my neck and slowly grazes his teeth along my skin. His lips are firm but soft at the same time. My back arches slightly hoping he will continue to place kisses on my skin.

It feels like I have been branded by him. What is left in his wake is a tingling sensation on the skin of my neck and the awareness that my panties are wet.

If I squirm, he will notice.

If I move, he will stop.

He looks down and slides his hands under my skirt over my fishnet stockings and up to my ass. "I can smell how wet you are for me," he says huskily.

My eyes close because, of course, a guy like Dravin can sense when a woman wants him. A man like him has a sixth sense. His hands squeeze my flesh, and he pushes me against him. His cock is hard underneath his jeans which only adds to my arousal. He wants me to know how I make him feel and he wants to make sure I feel it.

"Can you?"

I should tell him to stop. I should tell him to fuck off and get his hands off my ass, but another part of me can't get enough. I want to feel what it's like to be this close to him. To breathe the same air as Dravin Bedford for just a moment. With every breath he takes, I inhale the windstorm he is creating. The feel of his hands on my flesh and his hardness pressing against my belly is like a hurricane of heat blowing over my skin. I don't want to move. I want to stay right here in the dark and feel it for a moment longer. Then, I can go back to avoiding him.

My eyes are trained on his lips, and he licks them like I'm a meal he can't wait to taste. "Yeah," he breathes. The pads of his thumbs on each side of my hips make circles, causing my clit to throb with unbearable need.

This is all new to me. It's like he casts a spell every time I look into those smoldering eyes that make him look like he is possessed by something. Something dark that collects and takes parts of whatever he wants. The only thing you can remember is…that it was him who took it, but you would give it to him just to know he has a part of you.

What he wants from me, I don't know, but if he keeps touching me, I'm not sure I'll win the fight that is warring inside me. The good versus the bad. The good is telling me to run and never look back. The bad is telling me to give in and let him take what he wants, that I will enjoy it, even if it means I'll lose myself in the process.

My body shivers against him and he pulls me closer to his chest. My breasts press against his hard muscles and his hands pull me impossibly closer. A whimper escapes my throat.

"You want me," he says, his voice vibrating against my skin. "I feel it. I can feel how bad your pussy aches for me."

Fuck. I'm not very good at hiding how my body responds. My hands find the rough concrete behind me, feeling the texture to make sure I'm not dreaming.

He leans close and chuckles near my ear. "I'm not interested in girls that seem desperate, my little Raven. If you only knew how refreshing it is to find you aren't one of them."

Pushing off the pillar with my hands, he steps back, and his palms release me. The shadows cast from the light above make his features look maniacal. Why is he calling me his little Raven?

"Why are you calling me your little Raven?"

"That is what you are to me, my little Raven."

"You do know that Ravens eat dead carcasses and are an omen of death."

He shrugs. "If you say so."

I begin to walk away because I'm not sure if I should be insulted or flattered, but I know one thing for sure: I need to get away from him right now. He is all over me one minute, setting me on fire the next, and then calling me his little Raven the next. I can hear his footsteps coming closer behind me, but I keep looking straight ahead.

"Leave me alone, Dravin. Whatever happened back there should never have happened."

His footsteps become more distant as I approach the building and run up the stairs. When I'm finally in my dorm room, I sigh in relief, making sure the lock is secured. I pull out my phone and message Jess that I made it back, but after ten minutes of staring at my phone, she never responds. She probably hooked up with whoever caught her eye at that bar.

My thoughts go back to the cemetery and my encounter with Dravin. His expression is full of pain and faith, with an air of want and need but then restraint.

The guy came out of nowhere like an apparition. At first, I thought I was seeing things and had made it all up. One minute, he was at the bar near the billiard tables, and the next, he was behind me, questioning what I was doing alone in a dimly lit cemetery.

When he touches me, my body responds. Flames heat my

skin, making my heart skip a beat, and the tingling butterflies dance in my core. The dirty things he said have me wondering how it would feel to have sex with him. Will he be gentle or rough? Will he care that I'm not experienced? Will he laugh at me or reject me if he found out I'm a virgin, or would he be kind and teach me?

Even though part of me wants to find out, I just can't. Making up my mind, I'm determined to lay low and avoid Dravin Bedford at all costs.

CHAPTER SEVEN

DRAVIN

"HOW ARE you doing in school, Dravin?" my therapist, Dr. Wick, asks.

I lower myself in the seat across from her. "How's your niece doing?"

Her left eye twitches, but I give her credit for maintaining her composure. "I didn't ask that. Please stop redirecting the question," she says in a stern tone.

Her niece tried to overdose on painkillers after I fucked her. I had told her we would make it official, that we would be a couple, only to tell her the next day at a family function in front of everyone that she was delusional and should get help from a psychiatrist to treat her obsession with me.

It was my way of getting back at my father for requiring me to get therapy with Dr. Wick and having to sit there and watch her tell my father everything I said and what I had done. Obviously, patient confidentiality doesn't apply to Dr. Wick. I'm legally an adult, but if I don't get therapy, he threatens to report my other transgressions, and my plans to fuck over my father will go to shit. My father thinks I have a disorder. According to Dr. Wick, I have antisocial personality disorder (ASPD). I know she's full of shit and this is all my father's doing.

"It's going well," I respond dryly.

"Well? How about the casual sexual activity, manipulation, hostility, and deceit?"

She thinks that my environment triggers my actions. If she

only knew the families that founded the university were the ones with the problem. The families date back to the 1800s, when the university was first built near the church. The church is the center of everything. It is the perfect cover-up for the lies. Like a secret society, these families forge power and wealth. My father's side of the family is one of them.

I lean forward in my chair and give her a sarcastic smirk. "I have been a good little boy, Dr. Wick. There is nothing to report and there is nothing to tell."

"I see." She flips through the file in her hand, and I notice it's mine. "Professors at the university have not reported any issues regarding your behavior, though I have to ask about your relationship with Veronica."

"What about her?"

"Were you part of a scheme to ruin her relationship with that boy she was parading around with at last year's ball? According to individuals who were there, she had a break-down when he told her he just wanted to be friends."

"No. Why would I be?"

Veronica is the perfect daughter in everyone's eyes. If they only knew she is more fucked up than I am. Not that I consider myself to be fucked up. It's what everyone, including my father, says about me because they cannot control me.

My sole purpose in continuing this charade is to collect information. Dr. Wick gives me details that I need. Every session, I sit, listen, and redirect the questions back to her. I'm psychoanalyzing her and she doesn't even know it. All her questions are to see if she can take anything I tell her and run back and give it to my father. Not a chance. He wants to know everything before everyone. My father loves control and as one of the heads of our society, he needs it. He just goes about it the wrong way.

"Why do you feel you have to conduct yourself in the way that you do, Dravin?"

I chuckle. "Conduct myself how? I have sex. People your age consider that a problem, I don't. I fuck, Dr. Wick. I fuck a lot. It is healthy. I'm young, and if it is consensual, like with your niece, I get it done. That is not a problem. If someone pisses me off, I defend myself. I don't need to manipulate anyone. If I want something, I ask, and I usually get it. I don't force anyone to give me anything."

She knows I mean sex, and the jab about her niece is to rile her up so she ends the session. My father wants information because it's the beginning of the semester and things have been too quiet. It's unlikely for me to be quiet about the things I'm into and the things I want. Not for long, though.

"I think this session is over. We clearly have a difference of opinion. Your behavior hasn't been destructive as of late and there are no new reports."

"Am I cured, Doctor?" I mock.

"If the destructive personal behavior continues, Dravin, I'm afraid I will have to transfer you to another colleague."

"No need." I place the joint to my lips and light it with my zippo.

"There is no smoking in here, Dravin."

I blow the smoke in her face as I stand up to leave. "So you have said."

I inhale and blow more smoke in the air as I turn to leave.

"Leave, right now. And don't come back. I'll report this, and I will speak to your father." The phone rings interrupting her rant.

I'm walking out of her personal office and wink at the receptionist I fucked in the bathroom after Dr. Wick told me to wait in the waiting room before our appointment.

"Call me," she says, biting her lip.

"Dravin, that was the school," Dr. Wick calls out, but I'm already heading into the elevator, and the doors close, cutting off her annoying voice.

Fuck therapy. I don't need it and never did.

CHAPTER EIGHT

GIA

I'M SITTING through another lecture in my marketing class, and I just found out that Warren and some of the guys from the swim team are taking the same class. I'm hoping Warren got the message last Friday at the bar. When he turns to the side, I notice his hand is in a cast. My brows pinch into a frown.

Something must have happened over the weekend. Maybe he slipped and fell after he left the bar. He turns around, and our eyes lock, and I immediately glance away. Shit. He saw me looking in his direction.

He elbows the guy next to him and he turns around. I've never seen him before, but I notice him staring at me with a scowl. It seems he doesn't like me very much. He turns back around and faces the professor, and I shrug it off and pay attention to what the professor is lecturing about.

"Now, I'm going to call out group names so that you may exchange information for the marketing project due at the end of the term. It needs to be a social media ad campaign for any product. You will be graded on SEO, graphics, and the hook. It will make up twenty percent of your grade, so make it count."

He begins to call out student's names, and when Warren's name comes up, my stomach drops, and I suck in a breath. Let's hope he doesn't call out my name. When the professor calls another girl's name, I let out the breath I was holding relieved I dodged a bullet.

He paired him with a brunette named Jasmin. When I look over at her, she waves at Warren, and he scowls. He doesn't look very happy. He turns and glances at me once again and I guess he was hoping I would be paired with him. Too bad, buddy.

To my surprise, Warren raises his hand.

The professor pauses and looks up. "Yes, Warren?"

"Is it possible to change partners?"

The smile on Jasmin's face falls and she glares at Warren. He obviously isn't happy with the professor's choice. My hands begin to get clammy hoping that the professor is set on his choices.

"I'm sorry, Warren. Your partner for this assignment is whoever you are assigned to. There are no exceptions."

He dismisses Warren and continues to call out names. I finally look up when he says my name, but I wasn't paying attention to who he paired me with. My eyes widen when the guy who scowled at me gets elbowed by Warren and turns around, giving me a stare-down. He tilts his head and looks back at the professor when he is finished pairing up everyone in the class.

"The rest of class time can be spent exchanging information," the professor announces.

Everyone begins to move to their partners, but when my eyes land on my partner, he gets up and moves away toward the exit.

What the hell? I grab my bag and quickly run down the steps in the stadium-style auditorium. When I reach the door, I see his retreating back walking toward the exit.

"Hey!" I call out.

I didn't even catch his name. I run like a bat out of hell outside and squint from the sun's glare. Once my eyes refocus, they find him still walking away and I run to catch up with him. "Hey! Wait up!"

He stops and turns around. His eyes are dark, and once I reach him, I notice he is lean and tall. My head tilts up and he watches me, annoyed.

"What's your name again?"

He snorts. "Obviously, you weren't paying attention. It's Reid."

Shit. This must be the "*Reid*" Jess warned me about. I don't have a choice but to go through with it and have him as a partner.

"Well, Reid, I can't fail the class and we need to exchange numbers and figure this out." I pull out my phone from the back of my jeans and try to swipe to unlock it without cutting myself on the cracked screen. Shit. I'm upset, and I swiped a little too hard.

I gasp at the sharp stinging of pain. Snatching my thumb and placing it in my mouth, I hope I didn't get a piece of glass stuck inside the pad of my thumb. I suck but don't feel anything except the sharp sting.

Reid's lips form a thin line, and he grabs my phone out of my hand.

"Hey. What the hell do you think you're doing? Give me back my phone."

He ignores me and inspects the severely cracked screen. "It's fucked. You need to get a new one. It's not worth fixing the screen," he says, handing it back.

He pulls out his phone and it's the latest model iPhone.

"That costs money. Money I don't have right now, and no one is hiring until the holidays start. Even then, this place is in the middle of nowhere."

He continues looking at his phone and pulls up his text messages. "Try the library. What's your number?"

I rattle off the numbers and feel my phone buzz in my pocket.

"I'll text you my address. Meet me there at seven so we can go over the assignment."

"Alright, my name is—"

He finishes for me. "Gia, I know. Everyone…knows."

Lifting an eyebrow. "Everyone?"

"Yeah, and do yourself a favor. Stay away from—"

"Let me guess, Dravin." I interrupt him.

"I was actually going to say, Warren."

"Why not Dravin?"

I'm curious to know why he wouldn't warn away from the devil himself. The university's bad boy. Why would he warn me off Warren? Not that I don't agree with him.

His eyes scroll over me from head to toe. "You're not Dravin's type, and Warren is interested in you because everyone notices you. It will attract attention you are not capable of handling. I'm just trying to avoid a tragedy."

He means Veronica, but why would he say tragedy and not problem? Tragedy can mean death or destruction.

"Should I be worried?"

"Dravin wouldn't touch you. You are too… plain for his taste."

I'm too plain? Fuck him. I know I'm not sex on legs, but plain? I wear fishnets to a bar with a skirt. I'm not too thin or too fat. I think. I'm not fucking plain.

"I meant about Warren."

"If you're interested in Warren, run the other way. You might as well withdraw from the school and move far away because by the time she is done with you, you will wish you never set foot in this place."

We both know who he is talking about: Veronica. She can't be that bad. He turns around and dismisses me like I was just some random person asking for directions.

I have to say Reid is hot, mysterious, but a total ass. He has a terrible attitude problem. Then he insults me and tells me that I'm plain and that Dravin will not take me seriously. That I'm not his type. Fuck him. Fuck all of them.

———

The Uber drops me off on a street that has what looks like estates or what they call mini-mansions. I recheck the address, swiping my phone with a band-aid on my thumb, and it is definitely the right place. Who lives in houses like this two blocks away from campus? There are a total of six houses on this street and all of them have imposing gates that remind me of horror films. Each gate has a different gothic design scene. Like the house in Nightmare on Elm Street, House of Haunted Hill, and even Michael Meyers' house. I know they are not all mansions, but it is the scene. The feeling. These houses are all mansions, but they also all have something in common: they all look haunted and unnerving.

This particular house has many trees that hide its imposing size. A black gate leads to the cobblestone walkway because the one leading to the driveway is locked.

A gust of wind picks up the leaves off the ground signifying the beginning of the fall and reminding me I should've worn a heavier jacket. The gate closes with a click, and my heart begins to beat gallop, as if I'm walking into an impending doom.

The house isn't ugly, but it is overwhelming. It is white with black trimmed windows and gas-lighted lamps like the ones you see in New Orleans. I walk up the two steps that lead to the black wooden double doors. I'm about to press the doorbell when it suddenly opens, and Reid appears in the doorway.

"You're five minutes late."

"Normal college people like me don't have cars or live in huge houses near campus. We have to take an Uber, and I wasn't sure if I had the right address."

"How is that my fault exactly?"

"It isn't, but you don't have to be a dick about it. I haven't done anything to you, but you treat me like shit. I'm here to work on an assignment with you, not to hang out. Stop treating me like I'm here to fix the internet and I'm late. I'm not interested in anything else, and trust me, I'm not your type."

"What is your type?"

I snort. "The fact that all you remembered from what I just said is the part that you're not my type says a lot. Don't worry about it. Can I come in or not?"

He rolls his eyes and moves to the side holding the door open so I can come inside.

The place reeks of wealth. An interior decorator touched every inch of this place. This is not some house on frat row that was decorated by a bunch of college kids.

I wait for him to usher me to the area where we will be working. He closes the front door with a thud. The inside is decorated with light birch wood floors and furnishings in different shades of grey and black. The ceiling is lined with dark wood paneling, and there is a black marble-accented fireplace with white trim. The house is lit with a soft glow, and I think his family or whoever lives here prefers it that way. The curtains are luxurious floor-to-ceiling, covering the large windows that lead to a large pool that is lit up red, giving the impression that you are swimming in a pool of blood. Charming. Dracula must live here.

The home has an old Goth look mixed with a modern touch. It is definitely an old house that has been remodeled to fit modern times but has maintained the essence of its character.

Reid walks up the grand staircase, and I try to break the tension by complimenting him on his home, even though it's not all my style, mainly the lighting and the red pool.

"You have a very nice home."

He pauses on the landing and slightly turns his head. "It isn't mine. I just moved in here because my best friend was alone, and I didn't want to live with my parents. My parents' home is behind this one."

"Who's your best friend?"

He doesn't answer my question and I guess it doesn't matter. I'm just interested in getting the layout for the assignment and then I'm leaving.

The house is quiet and has no life except for the lights and the pool. It seems that no one lives here except Reid and his best friend because there are no family pictures anywhere—not on the walls or the credenza—nothing. Whoever his best friend is, they like solitude.

Following Reid down the hallway, he stops and opens the first door to the right. It is clearly a bedroom with a computer desk. My spider senses kick in because I thought we would go to an office or a loft with a desk and chairs we could work on, but not his bedroom.

His bed is massive, and it is the kind that has four posts.

My gaze falls on the dark sheets, and he notices where my attention is drawn to.

"Are you sure I'm not your type?"

"Positive," I quip.

He acts like a typical guy who's got a girl up in his room. Like every other guy in this place, he thinks I'm going to fall for his good looks. Most of the guys here can fool other girls and get them to do whatever they want. They must think I'm stupid because I didn't grow up here or come from money.

He smiles and sits at the edge of the bed facing me. I slide my bag, which carries my laptop and notebook, off my shoulder and walk over to place it on the chair in front of his desk.

"I like you, Gia. Not in that way. But—" He pauses and licks his lips. "Never mind. I'm just fucking with you. What do you have in mind for the assignment?"

My shoulders sag in relief and I let him know the ideas I have in my head on how a great marketing ad should look and what elements it should include.

"I'm just not good at the graphics part," I tell him.

"I'm good at the graphics part. I just need you to come up with the target audience and hook. I will put together the ad, SEO, graphics, and upload."

The computer on his desk is one of those gamer computers with RGB changing lights fading from one hue into another. He has a dock with various headphones, drives, and other computer-related accessories. He probably knows what he is doing and would be better at it than me since my laptop is old and on its last leg. It lags but gets the basic job done.

"Alright, fine. Sounds like a plan. What are we selling?"

He smirks. "What are you willing to sell?"

The door to his room suddenly is pushed open wider, and the last person I would have ever thought stands at the threshold, fury blazing in his eyes when he spots me standing in front of Reid.

"What the fuck are you doing in here?"

My eyes widen. "I—"

He doesn't let me finish or say anything. He grabs me firmly by the arm and pulls me out of the room into another room down the hall resembling his bedroom. He shuts the door and spins me around. My back is against the door, and he towers over me, caging me in. The corded veins over the muscles of his arms swirl under the ink of his tattoos. In the light of his room, I notice he has tattoos almost everywhere. I have never noticed them because he always wears long-sleeved sweaters or shirts. The only ones I could ever see are the ones that peek out from his neck and hands.

"Are you fucking him?"

I shake my head. "No, but it doesn't matter if I am or not. It's none of your business."

"You are in my house and everything that goes on here *is* my business."

Reid set me up. It is the only explanation as to why he failed to omit the fact that his so-called best friend is none other than Dravin Bedford. Now, I'm in his house and in his bedroom. When I take my next breath, all I smell is his cologne. Clean and fresh mixed with his tempting scent.

My chin lifts. "Look, I didn't know this was your house. Reid didn't tell me you lived here. I'm just here to work on an assignment and he is my partner. That's it. I think we were about finished. I can text him about it later."

Pushing myself off the door is no use because he doesn't budge.

"Move. I want to leave. I already told you why I was here."

His nostrils flare, but I'm not sure if it is due to anger or something else. It is hard to read his thoughts. He burns hot and cold, and I can't think around him. He confuses me. I'm angry with him one second, and the next, I want him.

"What's wrong? You don't want to see my room, my little Raven?"

"Why would I want to see where you bring your victims before you cast them aside." I nudge toward his bed. "I think I'll pass. I'm not interested in playing your games. I want to get my shit and leave. And stop calling me *your little Raven*. My name is Gia."

"To me, you are my little Raven. Get used to it. From now on, I'm calling you Raven."

Rolling my eyes, knowing there is no winning with him, I notice his massive king-sized bed, also with dark satin sheets and a grey comforter. His floors match the rest of the house, and he also has a desk but with three more screens than Reid.

His walls are bare except for three paintings I recognize. The first is Ary Scheffer's *Francesca da Rimini* painting, which shows a couple in lust. The second painting is John Collier, depicting Lilith with a snake wrapped around her body, known as a *demoness for thirst and revenge*. The third painting is of Francisco Goya's *Saturn Devouring His Son*, but if I remember correctly, the body being devoured is argued to look like a female instead of a male.

The three paintings remind me of the seven deadly sins. Why would he hang them in his bedroom? My eyes are so transfixed on the wall with the paintings that I don't notice he has stepped away, and I could easily open the door and leave.

"Which one do you like the most?" he asks in a husky voice.

My head snaps up to his like I was caught doing something I hadn't meant to be doing. My eyes fly across the paintings one more time and I honestly don't like any of them. My head tips up. "None. I don't like any of them."

He doesn't answer. He stays silent. He doesn't move. After a few more seconds, I turn and run back to Reid's room, thankful that his door is still wide open. When I enter to retrieve my bag, he is still sitting on the edge of the bed, leaning back with his elbows on the mattress. The knowing grin he is sporting makes the hairs on the back of my neck stand up. Prick.

"Whatever sick perverted game you two are playing, count me the fuck out," I snap.

The grin planted on his face tells me it wasn't a coincidence that I was paired with him for the assignment. How they managed to pull it off, I have no idea. The professor was firm that whoever you were paired up with was set in stone, and you couldn't change partners.

Reid doesn't move except for his eyes as he watches me collect my things and leave. He doesn't respond, and the silence tells me everything I need to know.

I'm in trouble, but I don't know how or why. All I know is that I'm a target for something. I just need to figure out what that is and who I need to defend myself from.

CHAPTER NINE

DRAVIN

"DID VALEN CALL?" I ask Reid when I walk into his room.

Gia left like her life depended on it. I was at a loss for words when she told me she didn't like any of the paintings. When I asked other girls I've had in my room, they always chose one. Then I ask them to leave my room. I never screw them on my bed. It is always somewhere else in the house. The couch, the pool, or the kitchen. Never in my room.

She is the first girl who has ever said she doesn't like any of them. This tells me something about Gia. She is innocent and pure-hearted, and I want to dirty her with my filth. The only problem is that I want to be the only one to do it.

"Ask me what you really want to ask and get it over with."

I'm looking around his room for some type of evidence to prove that they were only discussing the assignment for their class. A class he specifically signed up for at the last minute at my request. Call it my penchant for control, but I need to ensure I win.

My eyes fly to his. "Fine. Did you touch her?"

He gives me a hard stare. "Why? So I can look like Warren and fuck up the season. Coach is already ripping him a new one. Now we need Valen to step it up because of a bad temper and what happened to his arm. No thanks, I'll pass. I like my hands and need them to jerk off, swim, and fuck. It's not worth it. Not for a girl you will end up fucking anyway. I thought she was too plain or innocent for your liking? Why are you going to all this trouble? Just fuck her like all the other chicks that come through here and get it over with."

Reid, Valen, and I are the sons of the three founding families that founded the Kenyan University. Valen is a sophomore and the youngest of us. He is insatiable. The guy fucks like he is starving in the middle of the desert.

As for me, I've never fucked a girl for more than one night. One night of sinful pleasure is all I ever want and all I ever need. Otherwise, they all get clingy and expect more. That is when we play. We hurt. We destroy. We show them what they don't mean to us. We've always done it. Every girl. Every time. Except her. Gia will never be the target of our wrath.

I give him a hard glare. "Don't touch her, Reid."

He raises his hands. "I'll keep my hands to myself. Like I said, I don't want to end up like our buddy Warren. What did he do to deserve the wrath, Dravin?"

"He touched what he wasn't supposed to touch."

"Did he know that?"

"Not my problem if he does or doesn't. She obviously isn't interested. Now, he can't touch her with a fucked-up hand."

"I wonder what your dad and therapist will say?"

"Don't give a fuck because I'm not going to therapy anymore. Never needed that crap, and my purpose for going to therapy is done."

He remains silent, knowing not to keep fishing for more information I won't give him. I trust Reid and Valen, but right now, I'm annoyed that he brought her to his room. That wasn't part of the plan. I regret treating her the way I just did.

She ran out of here like the hounds of hell were right behind her.

I push off the door molding, looking at the time on my phone. "I need to go. Don't expect me back until morning."

"Where are you going?"

"To take care of my interests."

CHAPTER TEN

GIA

MY EYES SNAP open from a deep sleep. Something woke me, except when I look around the room, it's still basked in darkness. My eyes try to adjust, but the only light coming into the room is from under the door leading to the main hallway.

Jess and I share a room with twin beds on each side. A desk is placed at the foot of each bed, with two nightstands in between. One thing they never updated in this school is the dorms. There are the old traditional dorms you see in older schools.

I guess they don't have many students who need them. There are only forty students on each floor of the female building, and each building is only three stories. From what Jess has told me, there are only fifteen students housed on each floor in the male building. The rest live off campus or in frat houses. My eyes look around the room, but everything is so dark. I can't see much, but I wonder what woke me from my sleep.

Jess was already in bed when I walked in from Dravin's house. My hand reaches out to my nightstand to grab my phone, and I press the button so that the light can help me see around the room. When my phone lights up, I almost scream when a hand shoots out and covers my mouth.

My eyes widen in pure fear, but my fear begins to dissipate as I look into eyes that have been appearing in my dreams, along with a familiar scent that I quickly realize is filling my senses. His lips move silently, telling me to keep quiet. My head nods, not knowing what to do. Should I scream? My body makes up my mind for me because my nipples harden when his gaze drops to my soft cotton tank. He can see right through the fabric because of the bright light coming from my phone. When his gaze lingers, my nipples further betray me. When he takes my phone from my hand, the light shows his mouth turning into a frown, and he drops his hand from my mouth. He inspects the phone that looks like a mirror of broken glass. Some of the numbers and apps look smeared and unreadable.

He grips my wrist gently and notices the band-aid on my thumb. He unwraps it and I recoil my hand from his grasp.

"What are you doing here?" I whisper.

He doesn't respond and just watches me. He stares into my eyes and slides his fingers over my wrist again. The light on my phone shuts off, and we are once again enveloped in darkness.

He moves, and I can hear the rustling of clothing. Another light brightens my side of the room, and I see his hand holding his phone. He lifts my hand again and turns it over to inspect my thumb.

"What—

He places a finger on my mouth and mouths silently for me to be quiet. What is he doing here? Why is he here?

He shakes his head when he notices the cut on my thumb, and I know he can tell it's from the severely cracked screen of my phone. He places my phone back on my nightstand and motions for me to move over.

I shake my head, but he ignores me and lifts my comforter. My eyes dart to where Jess is sound asleep, and the light from Dravin's phone goes off and then back on. My gaze finds his, and he pushes me gently so I can give him room on the small twin bed.

My heart begins to beat, and my hands start to sweat. Dravin is in my dorm room after hours and is crawling into my bed. My head tilts up and he raises an eyebrow expectantly. Taking a deep breath, I move over to give him room and slide my hard, firm pillow over trying to fluff it up frustratingly. He grabs the pillow and throws it toward the foot of the bed, and I throw my hands up. *What the hell?*

He removes his shirt and I'm relieved the light from his phone turns off and the room darkens. If I see what he looks like with his shirt off, I don't know how I will be able to handle myself looking at him. He slides in next to me like we are a couple, and we have done this countless times. Like he is my boyfriend, and he sneaks in after hours all the time.

I'm sitting up and I'm stunned. My mind hasn't entirely caught up to the fact that Dravin is here and he is not leaving. My head turns and my eyes are trying to adjust to the darkness so I can look at his face. He moves, and it seems like he raises his arm, and I assume it's so I can lay on his chest.

My heart is racing, beating like it's going to rip out of my chest because I have never been in a bed with a guy before. I'm attracted to Dravin, but I don't know him. The only thing I know is that he is mysterious, a player, and ridiculously gorgeous.

"Relax, Raven. I'm not here to hurt you. Now go to sleep," he whispers so low I almost can't hear what he is saying.

I swallow, unsure of what to do. Should I get up and wake Jess and kick him out, or should I lay down and go to sleep on his naked chest and smile to myself that I have the hottest guy on campus wanting me to fall asleep next to him?

For once, I stop thinking and just do what my heart wants. I lay down and snuggle against his warm body with smooth skin and hard ripped muscle. My eyes close and I inhale the scent of his skin. I imagine that he is mine, and I am his. My skin vibrates everywhere he touches, and I mentally count all the places our bodies touch.

My lips curl into a smile. I'm not sure if this is real or if I'm dreaming. I just let myself feel and listen. His chest rises and falls. I know he is not asleep but still listening and waiting. My head tilts up to see if I can see the expression on his face. I want to figure out what he wants and why he is here. I try, but it's no use; it's dark, and my eyes are growing heavy. His breathing is steady and even. His body is warm and comforting. But I know he is awake.

Waiting.

Waiting for me.

Giving up, I turn my face, letting my cheek feel the smoothness of his chest. His fingers gently brush the hair from my face. It is so quiet, yet it's so loud. The beating of his heart thumps wildly but begins to slow down and my eyes drift closed. Listening to the beat of his heart and smelling the scent of his skin begins to lull me into sleep. I'm memorizing this moment because, right now, it is the only place I want to be. In Dravin Bedford's arms.

CHAPTER ELEVEN

GIA

MY ALARM GOES OFF, but my eyes remain closed. My mind begins to wake up, and then memories of last night come flooding back like a tidal wave. I bolt up from the bed and notice I'm alone. My eyes open, and I look around, wondering if it was all a dream and I imagined it. My alarm keeps going off on my phone and I silence it by pressing the side button.

Getting up from the bed, I look over, and everything appears like it was before I went to bed. I look over at Jess's bed. She must have gone to class because it is empty, and I notice her bed is made.

I shake my head. "It must have been a dream," I mutter.

After taking a shower and getting dressed, I head out of Drury Hall, where my dorm is located, and walk over to the main building for my math class. When I walk in, I take a seat in the far corner of the last row. I usually sit in the front in all my classes, but at Kenyan, with the type of college students that go here, I need to pay attention to not only the class but also the people around me. The back is where I can do both.

Something is not right about some of the people that go here. I just can't figure out what it is. Everyone looks at you like they know something you don't, and they will make sure you are the last one to find out and by the time you do, it's too late.

The professor walks in and introduces himself as Professor Walker. He looks middle-aged, but he's slightly built. His clothes are the same as most male professors—dress shirt, slacks, and loafers. He continues to introduce himself while he passes out the syllabus, and my mind tunes him out, going back to memories of last night. I'm still wondering if I made it all up or if Dravin is like Edward Cullen and shows up in girls' rooms unannounced in the dark of night. If it was real, how the hell did he get in? If it wasn't real, then I needed my head examined.

"Hey."

My head whips to my right and I see a guy giving me a smile. "Hi," I say and quickly look back to the front of the room. From the corner of my eye, I watch him as he continues to look at me with a wide grin. He knows I am looking at him even if my head is facing forward. I begin to tap my pen on my notebook. He has brown hair and brown eyes. He is good looking, like most of the guys I have seen around here. He's probably on the swim team. He has the same ripped body under a fitted shirt and pants slung low over his hips. His long legs are stretched out in front of him, and he keeps tapping his thumb on the desk.

He leans closer and whispers, "My name is Valen. You must be Gia."

My eyes widen. "How do you know my name?" I ask above a whisper.

He licks his lips and gives me a playful smirk. "A little bird told me."

Is this guy for real? Is this a joke? Smartass.

"You know it's not polite to keep secrets."

He smiles. "Who said I'm keeping secrets?"

"What do you want?" I snap.

I know I'm being a bitch, but I'm tired of the games.

"Relax. I just wanted to meet you since we are in the same class. I'm a sophomore, but I'm really good at math."

I suck at math, and I'm totally being a bitch right now, but the way he talks and the way he teases is both sweet and dark all at the same time. He said he is really good at math and is a sophomore taking calculus. Impressive. However, there is definitely more to him being in this class and sitting next to me. I can just feel it.

I'm feeling bad about the way I snapped at him just now. I'm moody and don't know who I can trust, but I can't think everyone who talks to me is out to get me. After forty minutes of silence, I sigh. "Look, I'm sorry I snapped at you."

"It's cool. I know I sounded a little weird, but I wanted to see for myself if the rumors were true."

"What rumors?"

He stays silent, and I think he isn't going to answer me. Whatever. There are ten minutes left in the class, and the professor is writing our first assignment on the board and telling us to get the required book for the class—a book I have not purchased yet.

"You are free to go," the professor says.

I collect my things and move to stand, making my way toward the exit. I pull out my phone to check the time, even though the last digit is a little blurry.

Once I'm out in the hallway, Valen comes up next to me. "You're even more beautiful up close," he says softly. He points toward the shattered screen of my phone. You need to get that replaced."

I pause, and he walks away without saying another word.

I'm even more beautiful up close?

I'm looking at my phone, smiling to myself, not believing I was paid a compliment. I'm pulling up the map on my phone, and I'm focusing on the shattered pieces to find out where the bookstore and the library are located. I can't replace my phone because I need the money I have for my books. Especially the math book. It is either the book or the phone, and I need the book or I'll fail the class. I remember Reid telling me to try the library, so that's where I head to first.

———

After I meet with the librarian, I have the biggest smile on my face. I was offered a job that would work around my schedule. Plus, since I work at the school, all my non-covered tuition is covered. Like my books. I will be reimbursed for any non-covered tuition expenses for this semester. All I have to do is pay for my food off-campus. The rest of the money can stay in my account. No more ramen noodles for me, and I can replace my phone.

When I get the chance, I have to thank Reid for pointing me in the right direction. The guy is an ass, but he saved mine. I'm walking across campus to Drury Hall. When I walk into my dorm, I stop. My mouth must be hanging open because my throat goes dry.

There is a small bag sitting on my bed with a sticky note stuck on it. I take a seat on my bed, pull the string to undo the ribbon, and look inside the bag. I pull out the white box with an Apple symbol on it. It is the latest smartphone, and the sticky note reads.

"Even in the dark, I fell right into you...and we fit perfectly."

Dravin

It was real. I didn't make it up. He was here. In my bed. And he held me... without his shirt on. I keep reading the sticky note over and over but put it away before Jess makes it back. Holding the white box with a brand-new phone inside, I realize I can't accept the gift. As much as I need it, I can't. It is too much, and now that I am able to replace mine, I can't accept it. I'm not sure if this is his way to get me to sleep with him, if he really likes me, or if he's just being nice, but the sneaking in, the phone, and the poetic note... He's getting to me, and I can't stop the feelings I'm having no matter how hard I try.

The door opens, and Jess walks in and sees me holding the unopened box in my hand.

"Hey, you got a new phone," she says, pointing at the box in my hand. "Whoa, that looks expensive."

I shake my head. "I didn't buy it. It was a gift."

She raises her brows. "Someone with deep pockets must really like you."

I lick my lips and ask her, "Hey, Jess. Did you wake up and leave the door unlocked last night after I went to bed? Did you hear anyone come in?"

I know I'm a chicken shit and should just ask her outright if she let Dravin in or if she knew he was here last night this morning."

She pinches her brows and shakes her head. "Um, no. I didn't hear you come in last night, but you were sleeping like the dead this morning. I made noise, but you didn't even stir. I'm surprised you woke up and made it to class."

Shit. How did he get in?

"Why? Is everything ok?"

I decide to tell her in case he does it again. I'm not sure if it was a one-time thing or not. Maybe he is testing me, or maybe he has done this with other girls, and she can tell me not to fall for it.

"He was here last night," I blurt.

I run my fingers through my hair and look at her. She's staring at me like I just spoke to her in a different language.

"I'm sorry. Who was here last night?"

I roll my eyes. "Dravin."

"Dravin?"

"Yes, Dravin. He showed up last night like Edward Cullen from Twilight and slept with me in my bed. It was creepy and hot all at the same time. Does he do that to get girls to screw him or something? Does he buy them shit he thinks they need?"

She blows out a breath. "Are you telling me he snuck in, fell asleep with you in the bed all night, and then surprised you by buying you a phone?"

"Yes," I say forcefully.

She walks around, pacing the room. After the fourth time going back and forth like she is doing suicides, she looks at me. "That is not like him, and I have never heard of Dravin buying anyone shit or sleeping in a bed with a female unless it's to fuck, and from what I have heard, never in his bed. Maybe he was hoping you would give it up."

"While you were asleep ten feet away? No way."

"You would be surprised what I have seen and heard around here."

"Like?"

"Like orgies and threesomes. It's not uncommon in college from stories you hear. It's just that these guys take it to a whole other level, and it has nothing to do with dating or liking a girl. They play games. Games that involve breaking hearts and questioning what is real and what isn't."

Is she serious? I have heard stories about frat parties and

college kids getting out of control, but what she is mentioning is a whole other level of fucked up.

"Jess, what you are saying doesn't sound that far off in the sense of a bunch of college kids breaking girls' hearts and sleeping with whoever they can. It does happen."

"Not when they do it for fun and don't care about the consequences. They don't care if you are in love with a boyfriend out of state or if you put up a giant iron wall. They will make sure to break you."

"Who's *they*?"

"The three sons come from the families that started this school, and the other kids their families deem." She makes air quotation marks. "Their circle of business friends and colleagues."

"Who are the three sons?"

"Dravin, Reid, and Valen."

My heart drops when the names rolling off her tongue are the three guys I have already encountered. Dravin showing up everywhere, Reid being my partner on an assignment, and Valen attending my math class. I start making shit up in my head. It can't be a coincidence. Can it?

"You've already met the other two, haven't you?"

I tell her how I have run into them. She nods, listening intently, though I can tell her head is spinning. The only thing I don't tell her is what he wrote on the sticky note.

"So, look. When there is an attractive girl, they see her as —" She trails off.

"What? They see her as—"

"A conquest. A game. A pawn like in a chess game. In this case, it looks like Dravin is the one who wants you the most for whatever reason. The only thing that is off, is him showing up here and buying you anything. He doesn't need to ever go to those lengths to sleep with a girl."

"Got it," I quip.

I kind of figured it was all bullshit. But hearing out loud that you are getting played... stings. The sticky note that is written by his hand is an ink of lies burning a hole in my bag. I want it to go up in flames. I would have preferred last night to be a dream. A glimpse created by my imagination. I realize that his words and gifts are like magic. And everyone knows that magic is a form of deception.

Anger begins to filter inside me. I snatch the bag off my bed and slide the phone inside it.

"What are you doing?" Jess asks me, her eyes going wide.

I hold the bag up by the strings. Two fingers curled under the handles. "What does it look like? I'm giving it back. He can shove the phone up the pin-sized hole of his dick."

Jess burst out laughing. "Fuck him. Just keep it."

"No," I deadpan, shaking my head. "No."

I get up and slide the bag inside my oversized school bag, gripping the sticky note and crushing it in my palm. I let it go so it can fall on top, swing the straps of my bag over my shoulder, and walk toward the door.

"Woah, woah. Where are you going?"

My hand is on the knob of the door, and I turn my head around. "Where does it look like I'm going—to Dravin's house."

"You're serious."

"Yes."

She gets up and throws a shirt over her tank top and slides her feet into her Vans. "I'm going with you for moral support. You can't go into the lion's den alone."

CHAPTER TWELVE

DRAVIN

"HAVE YOU FUCKED HER YET," Veronica asks as I hold my cell phone to my ear.

"I'm working on it."

She chuckles. "Losing your touch, Dravin," she drawls. "I never thought she would make you work for it. She isn't falling easily for your charms. Come to think of it, I should just have asked… Valen to do it and given it up to him instead. Reid and I don't get along very well."

My nostrils flare at her taunts. I don't lose, and I'm sure as hell not letting Valen touch her or….anyone. They have been warned not to get in the way until I'm done with her. All of us have an agreement. No fly zone until we say, or we are done with whoever we have our eye on. It usually takes no more than two weeks, but this is taking longer than I had initially thought.

"He's mad at you because you don't play by the rules."

"You're right, I don't. I break them. Let's face it. You don't follow them either. So there is that."

"Why are you calling me?"

"Because you're taking too long. I'm getting impatient."

I chuckle. "What's wrong, Veronica? Are you dying to ride my cock? You sound a little…desperate."

"Oh, please. You didn't think you could even go through with it. That little, small-town, emo bitch is not going to give it up that easily. She probably won't when she hears how you treat every piece of ass that has come your way." She sighs. "I hate to be the bearer of bad news, but I think you're losing this one. I'm just going to have to take care of her my way."

"You did enough with her roommate. She has probably told her what you did by now. They seem like they get along quite well. Reid is still pissed you went behind his back and set Jess up with Garret."

"Oh, please. Reid is a terrible loser. He is just mad that Garret and that other twit Melissa tasted her pootie before he had a chance."

Yeah, then you fucked him out of spite to make sure he wouldn't fall for the girl. Reid wanted her to himself for whatever reason, but Veronica the bitch wanted to play. Now everyone knows both Melissa and Jess play for both sides of the field. Veronica sent censored pictures to almost everyone on campus and made sure Garret told everyone Jess was a bad lay.

Everyone sees him in a different light because he has two chicks at once. He boasted about it in front of Reid, but he shrugged it off like he didn't give a shit. But I know better; Reid doesn't like people to get in the way of his plans. His plan was to seduce Jess and fuck her every way he wanted before anyone else could. She attacked Gia, so now I'm going to get her where it hurts her the most.

"Whatever, how's Warren treating you?"

I know he is still avoiding her like the plague. He has been going around saying that the girl he was dating is a sex-crazed basket case. There is nothing that she can do that will change his mind. The guy's mind is already made up about her, but to a disturbed bitch like Veronica, I'll keep that to myself. If I tell her, she will go on the warpath. I don't have time to deal with spoiled little rich brats like Veronica. My father and then her father will want me to clean her mess up. Not happening.

It is better to avoid it altogether and hope she finds new Prey and forgets about Warren dismissing her.

She huffs on the phone. "Very funny, like you don't know."

I chuckle. Jasmin decided to giggle at that exact moment. My head whips around. Jasmin is on her knees on the sundeck of the pool, giving both Valen and Reid blow jobs. While I'm outside walking by the edge.

"Is that who I think it is giggling? Don't tell me you didn't participate."

"Nah, Reid and Valen wanted to play."

Jasmin takes Valen and Reid's cocks into her mouth, taking turns deep-throating them as they grunt and each of them has a hand fisting in her hair. Veronica wanted to make sure Jasmin was taken care of since we were the ones to pair her with Warren.

"Nah, she isn't my type. Too easy. She didn't even make it interesting."

"You're a sick bastard. Do you know that?"

I'm watching as Jasmin slides her mouth up and down Valen, then Reid, and back again. She slides her fingers down and plays with herself, and I sit watching the show.

She pulls Reid's cock out of her mouth. "He's watching me," she says.

"He likes to watch sometimes."

"He doesn't want to join?"

"Hey, Dravin, we got a thirsty one," Valen calls out, tilting his head like he can't believe Jasmin is down to suck all three of our cocks. "I kinda like her."

Her eyes look up and she smiles at his praise.

"I'm good right here," I tell them.

I'm not interested in having Jasmin suck me off. This definitely has Veronica written all over it. She made sure Jasmin was up for it.

"What did you do?" I ask Veronica.

"Making sure she doesn't suck the wrong cock or, in this case…cocks."

"How do you know she hasn't already?"

She means Warren. According to Reid, Jasmin has been partnered with Warren and he made sure it happened that way. It is his way of playing games. He knew Veronica would want us to take care of Jasmin. She had little hearts in her eyes when she was partnered with Warren. Reid said Warren was hoping to be partnered with Gia. He was boasting about how lucky Reid was that he was close to the girl no one has been able to fuck.

"Don't worry. I know." She snickers in that annoying way she does. "It's just added protection. Reid or Valen will boast about it in the locker room after practice."

"Whatever. Is that all?"

She makes a noise like she is stretching. "Yes," she purrs. "Make sure you guys clean up the stains of your sins." She laughs and I hang up.

"Crazy, bitch," I mutter.

I grab the towel and dry myself after the swim I had before I answered the phone. Jasmin has decided to show Reid and Valen how deep her throat is. I pick up my shirt to head inside, ignoring the noises and grunts coming out of the three on my pool deck. Then I suddenly realize that Jasmin is boring and takes too long to please.

CHAPTER THIRTEEN

GIA

"HAVE YOU BEEN HERE BEFORE?" I ask Jess, closing the door of her Honda.

She parks on the side of the street, and I'm thankful she decided to tag along and save me the cost of an Uber.

She shakes her head as we head to the open gate that leads to the walkway. "No. Never. I have heard of the street the three sons of the founding families live on, just like everyone else, but I have never actually been to any of their houses. They usually hang out at the bar or at the frat houses."

We walk side by side until we reach the massive door. The sun is beginning to set, leaving the sky with streaks of purple and grey and the air is getting cooler. It will be just another week before the temperatures begin to drop. Right now, it gets hot during the day and cooler at night. The leaves on the trees are starting to turn a shade of brown and fall off leaving the sticks of the branches like swirling veins.

I grip my bag to my side, making sure the strap doesn't slide off my shoulder. "Thanks for coming," I tell her.

"Trust me. I want to see the look on his smug face when you give it back. I couldn't let you come here alone when you are so pissed. I would be too if I knew what I know now. These guys have a motive for everything. Everything has a purpose, and they Prey on girl's feelings. At the same time, you can't blame them. I mean, who wouldn't want the attention of a hot guy or the chance to sleep with them. Some girls don't even care how they're treated as long as they can have a chance."

I figure what she is saying is the truth. It seems that way, and guys like Dravin are skillful manipulators. You get sucked in by their words and forget that you are just another name in a long list, and before you know it, you're giving yourself up too easily. The war between emotion and reason, like the line between love and hate, becomes blurred. In the end, all that is left is hate because your pride has silenced you into tears.

I don't knock. I just turn the handle of the massive door and watch it open. Nervousness coursing through my veins. My hands shake as I think about the confrontation that must ensue, but Dravin leaves me with little choice, and right now, I couldn't care less if he isn't expecting me. I came to return the so-called gift and note but haven't thought about what I am going to say when I see him or how he will react to me being in his house again. Will he be happy or pissed?

Jess follows me as we walk down the hallway. Everything is the same as the last time I was here, except there is movement behind the kitchen island leading out to the pool. The sun is setting behind the massive windows as the shadows of four people come into the dimly lit house.

The girl partnered with Warren in my marketing class makes an appearance, fumbling with her fingers to tie the straps of the bottom and the top of her bikini. The two pieces of fabric covering her nipples hang loose over her small breasts. It's obvious she was recently naked.

Jess pauses right beside me as Dravin comes inside, pulling a t-shirt over his flawless body and hiding the swirls of ink on his chest and torso. My heart begins to pound not in want or need, but in anger. Anger because of the lies spilled in ink left on a piece of paper. Anger because the girl he chose to be with at this moment is not me. I shouldn't be feeling this way, but I do.

Two more figures come into the light. Reid and Valen appear, and the puzzle pieces fit perfectly. Everything Jess has said rings inside my head like my alarm waking me up every morning. I'm thrown back into reality from the darkness of my dreams.

Reid has his swim trunks slung low on his ripped frame, and so does Valen, a younger version of the three with a similar build. They are heartthrobs with perfect faces and bodies who steal hearts like thieves in the night, leaving behind tears in their wake.

"What are you two doing here?" Reid is the first to ask, his voice hard and sharp.

He is clearly unhappy that we have shown up and entered the house unannounced.

I finally swallow and find my voice. Jess is frozen in place, shooting lethal daggers at Jasmin. She smirks at us with a knowing smile, adjusting her swimsuit like she is the luckiest girl on the face of the earth, and we just discovered her secret.

Jasmin's lips turn up into a smile laced with sarcasm. "You're the girl in my marketing class." Her eyes land on Jess. "Aren't you the girl that slept with Garret? I'm really sorry about what happened. He shouldn't have outed you like that."

What a bitch.

At first, I was feeling sorry for her, but now I hope they make a point of ruining this girl. She probably just had a threesome and now is redirecting her vitriol by pointing out what happened with Jess.

"I didn't come to see you." I nudge my chin and lift it

toward a silent Dravin. I came to see him."

My eyes land on Dravin and his expression is hard. His light eye twitches slightly. He is obviously annoyed that I'm here, so I decide to make this quick.

"This is going to be interesting," Valen says, crossing his arms over his ripped chest.

"Good. I was hoping it wasn't about school," Reid chimes in.

Valen raises an eyebrow to Jasmin. "You can see yourself out."

Her face falls and I smile. "Hey, Jasmin." I make a motion to the corner of her mouth." You might want to wipe the corner of your mouth. Your desperation...It's dripping."

She glares at me as she grips her bag. She shimmies into her shorts and forcefully slides her sweater over her head. Valen chuckles when she glowers at me, and Jess huffs her way toward the front door.

"Thanks for stopping by," Valen calls out after her.

Reid glares at Jess as he moves toward the stairs. "What the hell is she doing here?"

"I came with her, but don't worry, we're not interested in staying," Jess retorts.

"Good because no one invited you two. Especially... you. I'm not interested in being around someone else's scraps," Reid snaps.

Jess's nostrils flare, and I know he is talking about her falling from grace with Garret. It is messed up that he throws it in her face when he has probably done worse.

"Funny, you were interested in hearing all about it before," Jess volleys back.

Reid's lips curl into a snarl while climbing the stairs. "What's wrong, Jess? Jealous."

Jess snorts and claps her hands together. "Yeah, because you are such a fantasy. Just what a girl dreams about—a guy that has stuck his dick in more holes than a drill. Please."

Valen bellows in laughter at their back-and-forth while Dravin is still standing motionless on the other side of the marble island in the kitchen. It's like he didn't hear the banter between Jess and Reid or even Valen telling Jasmin to leave. He is standing like a spectator, watching everything unfold, with not an ounce of emotion on his face.

He watches me with his arms hanging by his sides. My heart begins to beat in my chest harder than it should. I'm suddenly aware of every breath and swallow I take. The phone he gifted me and the note sit like bombs in my bag. We just stare at each other, and my eyes gaze into his like I'm looking out a window. One eye is like the sunrise, and the other is like the sunset. Light and dark. Night and day.

Every time he is in a room, I'm aware of him. It doesn't matter if it's full or empty, I feel his presence. It is always him I remember and the only one I cannot forget. He continues to watch me as I walk forward and slide the strap of my over-sized bag off my shoulder. I take out the gift bag and place it on the counter. My head tilts up, and I swear he flinches. I slide my hand over the scrunched sticky note and slowly lift my hand in a fist and open it over the bag. His eyes follow the small piece of paper as it rolls over the side of the gift bag until it lands on the counter.

Our eyes meet and no one speaks. From the corner of my eye, I see Valen and Jess leave the kitchen and walk toward the living room, leaving us alone.

My tongue slides over the front of my teeth while my mind is trying to find the right words to say. The right words that need to hide the way I'm feeling about him screwing someone today when last night he had his arms wrapped around me like a blanket. Then the anger takes over because he must think I'm just some stupid girl from the middle of nowhere that he can take advantage of.

He moves forward, looks at the crumbled note, and meets my eyes. My eyes get glassy, and I get emotional because, for one moment, I wanted to believe it was real.

That he wanted to be in my bed.

That he cared that I needed a new phone and knew I couldn't afford one.

That it pained him to see that I cut myself on the broken glass on the screen.

That he meant those words on that piece of paper.

The devil must exist because, otherwise, someone couldn't be so beautiful and so cruel at the same time.

I keep my voice low. "I know you must think I'm stupid or that I'm some girl who can easily be taken advantage of, but I'm not. I don't need you to buy me anything. I don't want anything from you. I would rather cut my fingers off than accept something from someone who lies and deceives people."

A slow smile creeps up his face before he answers. "Did I ask you to sleep with me last night? His eyes drift up at the ceiling as if lost in thought. "Did I? Did I ask you to sleep with me this morning?"

"I'm not like that tramp that just left here, or any other girl you secretly screw around with. Your looks and tattoos and mysterious charm don't impress me."

He leans on the counter and acts impervious to my rudeness. "Calm down, Raven. I'm just trying to be your friend. Sure, I find you attractive, and I like you, but I didn't mean to buy you a new phone so I could get something out of you.

You needed it. It was a friendly gesture. I know I came on to you, but it is what I'm used to, and you've already expressed to me that you are not the type of girl who just sleeps with a guy who gives you the right attention." He points to the bag. "Take the phone."

"No."

"Take it. How else am I to call you without worrying you'll slit your finger when you answer?"

"Why would you call me?"

He shrugs. "I don't know. Maybe I want to ask you to go with me somewhere as friends. Maybe I could take you where you need to go if Jess is unavailable. I noticed you don't have a car. Things like that. We can hang out."

I find this side of Dravin really weird. Is he for real, or is he trying too hard?

"You don't have to go through all this trouble, you know. I'm not going to sleep with you, so you can quit while you're ahead and save yourself time."

"I'm serious, Raven."

My brows shoot up. "Why are you being so nice to me, and why do you keep calling me Raven?"

I begin to fidget with my hair, running my fingers through the long, dark strands. I'm curious to know why he keeps calling me Raven.

"Did you know ravens mate for life? They represent prophecy and insight. They are highly intelligent, and they eat anything they want. They can survive in the face of danger and are considered spirit animals. They date back centuries. Most people think they are a bad omen, but that could be further from the truth. Seeing one is actually good luck. Ravens are beautiful birds with black wings just like your hair."

"You think all those things about me?"

He nods. "Yes, I do." He walks around the island and leans close. "There are a lot of things I think about that remind me of you, and there are a lot of things I want to know about you, too."

His face is a few inches from mine, and I can smell the scent of pool water mixed with his cologne. His dark hair is spiked up and wet. His nose piercing is still in, and his eyes are tracing my lips.

His lips lean close, and I swear he can hear my pulse beating in my neck. "I didn't sleep with Jasmin. I never touched her. She wasn't here for me," he whispers.

I can't breathe. The fanning of his breath on my skin raises goosebumps over my flesh. The hairs on the back of my neck stand up like he is a magnet pulling them. It's like he has me in a trance when he pulls away and stands up to look down at me. His eyes caress my face. The only thing I can hear or feel is the sound of us breathing.

"I have to get back. Jess is waiting for me in the living room, and she's my ride."

"Oh, right." He turns toward the counter and slides the box out of the bag. His other hand reaches and takes the note, smoothing the paper I scrunched up in my hand.

He hands it to me slowly. "Please accept it. I know you have heard things about me, and most of them are true, but not all. They come from people who don't really know me."

Feeling a tad guilty that I accused him of screwing Jasmin, I take the box and slide it into my bag. He hands me the note. "I meant what I wrote."

He sticks his hand out for me to shake. "Friends?"

I sigh dramatically and slide my hands into his. "Friends," I say softly.

His eyes light up and he grins. He clears his throat. "I'll walk you out."

"Ok."

We walk down the hallway, and I can hear soft laughter and Jess's giggle from the living room. She is seated really close to Valen, and her eyebrows rise when she sees Dravin behind me. "Ready?" she asks.

I glimpse from the tiny smirk on Valen's face to Dravin. "Yeah."

When we reach the front door, Dravin softly grips my wrist, halting me. I turn my head and look at him. "My number is written inside the box of the phone. Call me to let me know you guys got home safe?"

Jess's eyes go wide like saucers. I don't think she has ever seen Dravin act this way with anyone before.

"Okay, I will. Bye…and thank you."

He leans close and gives me a soft kiss on the cheek that warms me on the inside. It is a friendly peck, but to me, it feels more intimate. It feels like the beginning of something I can't describe. I came here to throw a gift in his face and tell him to forget me. I'm leaving with the memory of his words and promise of friendship and a lot of feelings that I can't even begin to process.

CHAPTER FOURTEEN

DRAVIN

CLOSING MY LOCKER DOOR, I see a set of eyes belonging to Warren. My annoyance rises to unsafe levels because I'm questioning everything regarding Gia. The reasons I'm pursuing her are blurring into uncharted territory. At first, it was because I refuse to lose and love a challenge. I like to win. Especially when Gia is something I am interested in anyway. I have been drawn to her since the first time I laid eyes on her. The fact that I can get to this prick is a bonus.

There is just something about Warren even looking at Gia that rubs me the wrong way. I'm not used to being jealous of a girl, but for some reason, I want to hurt every guy who looks at her. When it comes to Warren, it would take a sexed-crazed basket case like Veronica to scare him off or someone like me.

"You ready?" he asks.

"I'm always ready?"

I'm the best on the team. As a senior, I have been offered a spot on the international team. I have the stats, the athleticism, and the drive. I practice every day, and that's why I prefer to live alone in my own house. I allowed Reid to move in because his father pressures him about taking over the family business. The pressure affects his swimming, which isn't good for any of us.

The three of us, Valen, Reid, and myself, have overambitious fathers who are driven by money and power. They groom us to maintain powerful relationships and tell us that when the time comes, we will choose a wife out of convenience. The only problem is that your moral lines become blurred when you're thrust into an environment like that. Everything becomes physical satisfaction. Your emotions are only sacrificed if you lose, so you learn to never lose.

I'm walking out to the pool, ready to compete and win. I want to see the look on her face when she sees me at my best. There is only one thing I care about—the only thing my father didn't take away from me—my love for competitive swimming. "Hey, when I walked in, I saw Gia sitting in the stands."

I pause and notice Reid and Valen pass by, overhearing the dickface in front of me. "What about her?"

He uses his fingers on his good hand to adjust the band of his swim shorts that are on his skinny, lean frame. He shrugs and gives me a smirk. "I heard you two are just friends."

"And your point? You need another reminder with your other hand?

"Hey, let's go. Coach is waiting for us, and if we head out too late, we will be swimming laps until we throw up," Valen chimes in. trying to diffuse the annoyance that must be written on my face at the mention of Gia being my friend.

Warren's eyes widen. Now he knows why I pushed him hard enough to fall and break his arm at swim practice. He thought it was because I was annoyed that he elbowed me by mistake when he was horsing around with another guy on our team. He knows it's about Gia, and I might just have to wipe that smug look off his face.

"Look. I don't know what your deal is, but I do know that she isn't the type of girl you are used to having fawn all over your dick. I am just wondering if your intentions are of the good variety. I don't want the same thing to happen to her, just like it happened to her roommate Jess. Veronica has a mean streak, but I'm sure you already know that, and I like Gia. She seems like a really nice girl. I would hate for something to happen to her by associating herself with the wrong people."

My lip curls. "Are you telling me to stay away from Gia?" I step closer, my fist clenching, my knuckles turning white. The strap of my goggles crushes against my palm. "Let me guess, you're the type of guy that would treat her right. A skinny prick with a small dick and a trust fund."

He steps back. Fucking coward. He knows I will slam his face against the door just to see his nose splatter all over the place.

"We'll see, Bedford. It isn't like you to make friends with the new girls who come through here who won't fuck you. Especially the kind that live in the dorms. I wonder what your father would think?"

I lunge at him, but Reid grabs my hand and pulls me back. "He isn't worth it, Dravin," Reid says softly.

Warren chuckles as he walks away. "You did always have a bad temper, Bedford. Relax, it's not like she will last anyway. Sooner or later, she will be riding someone's cock." He shrugs. "They all fall Prey to our charm and good looks eventually. It's who can get it first—that's the fun part. Sucks for you she friend-zoned your ass."

"Piece of shit," Valen spits. "I hate that motherfucker. He's lucky his father is in our circle. If not, I'd be the first one to drown his ass."

I shrug out of Reid's hold. "That makes the three of us. Make sure he stays away from Gia. The last thing we need is Veronica on her, too."

"How about Jess?" Reid asks.

"I'll let you deal with her since you two get along so well."

"Come on, let's go give them a show. I hate Ohio State.

The girls have a lousy head, and the guys on the team think they can beat us every year," Valen says.

"You need to chill, Valen. Your dick is gonna fall off."

"You're just jealous that I'm getting more pussy than you are right now because you have a hard-on for your little Raven. What can I say? I have an appetite, I like pussy."

I shake my head, knowing he is just being the way he is. He's the youngest one out of the three of us with the biggest appetite for screwing whatever catches his eye, but make no mistake, Valen is dangerous in his own way. He just respects me and sees me like the big brother he never had. He won't touch what's mine. Someday when he finds his, he will understand.

CHAPTER FIFTEEN

GIA

I FOLLOW Jess to an open spot in the stands. The smell of chlorine swirls around us in the enclosed Kenyan pool center. There is hardly a seat available. This is one of the top sports at the university.

"Are you ready to see the guys in all their delicious glory?" Jess teases.

"I have never been to a swim meet before."

"You're kidding?"

"Nope. My parents are churchgoers. They aren't into sports. I chose Kenyan because my mother thinks I'm following God."

She snickers. "It's that bad, huh?"

"How else was I to convince both of them after their divorce to let me move to another state."

"No shit. That is crazy. If they only knew this place has nothing but sinners."

"Yeah, I used to think they went to church because they lived this pious life, but it was all a lie. Look at my dad. He cheated on my mother, and then she asked to divorce him. Where was God?"

"Tell me about it. This was the only place that I could get a scholarship besides Ohio State. I wanted a better education at an Ivy League school. My mother had me young and worked at a bar. My father split before I was born, and it was just me and my mom and all the random boyfriends throughout the years. I'm trailer trash where I come from. At least my mom isn't a drug addict or anything. We're just poor."

I nod. Listening to her story makes mine look like rainbows and unicorns. At least I know who my dad is, and I lived in a stable home until after I reached adulthood. I don't come from money, and my parents lived paycheck to paycheck. The only thing they lied about was how they really felt about each other. They hid it well by going to church twice a week to cover up the truth. I know now that most people, even my parents, are liars.

People begin to clap as both teams come out of the locker room for the competition to begin. The Olympic-sized pool has a total of eight lanes and is divided into two sections. My eyes seek Kenyan's swim team, and I immediately see the only reason I'm here, Dravin. I admire his flat stomach, double-wide shoulders, and well-defined biceps under his tattoos. The way his swim shorts stick like a second skin makes my thighs press together. His thick dark hair is still dry, and he hasn't put on his swim cap yet. He is sexy as hell.

A girl on the women's swim team saunters up to him and a pang of jealousy hits me when he smiles at her. The smile she gives him in return has me determined to look away and find anything else to concentrate on. I instantly regret my decision because the last person I want to see is smirking my way and waving his free hand while the other is enclosed in a white cast. Warren.

I try to look away, but he keeps waving at me. "Great," Jess mumbles.

I glance at her, and next to her is a pissed-off Veronica glaring at Warren. I rip my eyes away and land on the blonde with porcelain skin. Her gaze is boring into me like she wants to rip my heart and eyes out.

She gives me a sarcastic smirk, but I play it off. "I think he's trying to get your attention," I tell her.

She looks over and aims her best smile at Warren. His change in demeanor and the way his face hardens says it all to everyone watching. It wasn't her attention he was trying to get.

"Well played," Jess whispers as Veronica gets up.

At least he won't be looking over here. I hope she sits below us so he won't be tempted to get my attention again. Luck is on my side, and she sits in his direct line of vision to where Jess and I are seated.

I glance over at where Dravin was standing and my heart sinks. The beautiful female swimmer is back and laughing at something he said despite his serious face. His dark lashes make him look like he is wearing eyeliner. He is just so gorgeous to look at. It is like God or maybe the devil took his time when creating Dravin.

His eyes find where I'm seated in the stands, and we stare at each other. The girl is rambling off about something, but his eyes are trained on me. He doesn't wave or smile. I wave at him slightly, but he just stares and something dark passes over him. Something dangerous, and I realize it was a mistake coming here. I thought it was what he wanted. He asked me to come because he wanted to be my friend, but something has changed.

His expression is dark. Both eyes are almost the same shade, if that's even possible. He forcefully plasters a smile on his face and looks at the girl with her perfect body in a one-piece swimsuit. His gaze lands on her breasts and he smiles at her.

Having had enough, I get up. My emotions are all over the place. I have never felt jealousy before, so this is all new to me. I should have never agreed to be his anything. This is stupid, and I should take everyone's advice and stay far away from him.

"Where are you going?" Jess asks, a concerned look on her face.

"I'm leaving. It was a mistake for me to come here," I tell her.

She looks up with wide eyes and then glances over at Dravin and then back at me. He is still standing near the girl, and she touches him on his muscled chest. He doesn't make a move for her to remove her hand. He leans close and whispers something in her ear and her cheeks smolder.

"That's Warren's sister. She always flirts with Dravin or Reid. Even if her brother doesn't' approve, you can't blame the girl for trying," Jess says.

This isn't going to make me feel any better about the whole situation.

I grab my bag and move before the meeting starts and people hunker down in their seats. "You can stay. I don't think he needs me to be here for moral support. He has enough fans." I look over and spot Veronica, with her eyes still focused on Warren and his expression of pure hatred while he watches Dravin and his sister chatting it up. "I think I should go."

"Are you sure?"

I nod. "I'm sure. I'll be in the library. Find me there when you're done here, and we can go and get something to eat. I start my job there on Monday, and I need to get a feel for where everything is."

She nods. "Okay, I'll see you in a bit."

———

I'm walking through the door of the library, and it feels old. Ancient. It smells of books and construction paper. I always thought certain books smelled just like construction paper. Especially the cream-colored interior of some of the books I've read. I love to open them up and smell them before I begin. When Reid mentioned working at the library, it was like a blessing in disguise. I notice there are statues of gargoyles in the library and vines on the ceiling on dark gold baroque paper. The desk is dark wood with stained glass, lighting the area in a colored glow. It's dark but lit in all the right places.

I glance at the checkout desk and notice a young guy with straight brown hair and amber eyes. He is nice-looking, I would say, in an Abercrombie kind of way.

"Hi, you're the new girl. You start Monday, right?" A young, handsome guy in ripped jeans says, seated in the front.

I look around and notice we are the only people in here. I guess the library on campus is not a popular place on Fridays.

I slide my hair behind my ear and clear my throat. "Yeah, I'm the new girl."

He moves his brown hair away from his face. His amber eyes meet mine. "That's great. I am glad they finally hired someone. There aren't many students who attend Kenyan who need a job. Most of them don't ever need to work, much less attend school."

"I see. I guess that makes sense."

He smiles, and his expression is warm and airy. He seems pleasant.

"Have you worked here long?" I ask him.

He moves around the desk, and I notice his ripped jeans and lean build. I'm not surprised. All the guys who attend here have good looks and killer smiles. With money or without, it doesn't matter. It's like they picked all good-looking students out of high school and threw them all into one elite university.

"Since, last year. I got in on an academic scholarship during my freshman year. I needed a job, and the perk of this one is that you get your other expenses covered. My mother lost her job at the end of my sophomore year."

"That must have been hard. Where are you from?"

"Small town in Kansas. You?"

"Wisconsin."

"I guess I don't feel so bad not being from a big city now that you're here."

I give him a grin. It's refreshing to find someone normal for once. So far, Jess is the only normal person I've met. Everyone else avoids me or gives me side glances like they are waiting for something to happen. I just don't know what that something is.

"I didn't catch your name."

"Gia."

"Is that short for something?"

I smile. He is the first person who has asked. "It's short for Gianna."

"That's a pretty name. I like both versions of it." He whips his hair from the side of his face. "My name is Marc, by the way." He shifts forward and gestures to the bookshelves. "Since you are already here, I'll give you the grand tour. I thought you would be at the swim meet to watch the sons of Kenyan."

I pause and furrow my brows. "Who?"

"The sons of Kenyan." He rolls his eyes and stretches his arms, making his T-shirt ride up, showing a flat stomach. "I'm sorry. I have been sitting for a while reading up for my poetry class on Monday."

"You're taking poetry? It's an elective. It didn't start the first week of the semester because the professor couldn't make it."

His eyes smile. "How do you know about that? Are you taking that class, too?"

I nod. "Yeah. It is a solid choice for me. I like reading poetry and prose."

"Same. It's not common for guys to like it, but I do. To answer your question, the sons of Kenyan are three guys on the swim team: Dravin, Reid, and Valen. Their families founded the university and built it around the Catholic Church of Kenyan. I'm sure you have heard of them by now."

"Yeah, unfortunately, I have two of them in my classes so far. I've just never heard of them being called the sons of Kenyan before. Reid in marketing and Valen in Calculus. To make matters worse, I have Reid as my partner for an upcoming marketing project."

"I feel bad for you. I wonder how they manage to have time for school with all the girls they go through."

I stiffen because that means Dravin is also part of the "*they*" he is referring to, but I have decided to get over that jerk. He is definitely playing with me. The way he dismissed me at the swim meet moments ago by openly flirting and gawking at another girl like I didn't even exist... stung. Why can't he be friendly and outgoing like Marc?

I'm glad Marc shows me around the library so I know where everything is located. As we walk down every aisle, he points out things I need to know in every section. The computers, the system for checking books out, and how to process everything are seamless. Even if the library looks like it's a hundred years old, it is equipped with the latest technology.

"Here." He hands me a thick, leather-bound book. It's the history of Kenyan University. Read up on it. It will make sense of everything. You just have to read between the lines," he says in a serious tone.

It's like he is trying to tell me something without telling me. Like he is talking in a secret code.

"Okay," I say, taking the heavy book in my hand. "Hey, what about the church?" I ask curiously.

He stops and leans against the front desk. He takes a deep breath, like he is choosing his words carefully. "The church seems just like every Catholic church that has its mass on Sundays and confession. But there have been stories since it was built, even before the university was built around it."

I'm intrigued by the university, the church, and the fact that Dravin is one of the sons of Kenyans.

Marc lowers his voice, and I find it strange, but I'm so curious I overlook his nervous behavior. It's like he doesn't want anyone to know he is telling me anything about its history. "Supposedly, the church was built and is used by a secret society of rich and powerful men. Men who are in politics, who come from influential families with power and money. They use the church as a meeting ground to discuss what they needed to do to control their businesses, people, and the government. There are members of this group, and they are all men. Their women are chosen by their pedigree and lineage. Marriages of convenience and never of love. They have to produce an heir. Male or female, it doesn't matter. The members are allowed to sin but would use the church as a cover-up. It is a church but not a real church."

"What do you mean allowed to sin?"

He swallows, and I tilt my head and watch as he looks to the door and then back at me. He checks his phone for the time and continues. "Did you read the bible when you were a kid or go to church?"

"Yeah," I answer quietly.

He closes his eyes like he is telling me something he shouldn't. "Supposedly, they don't follow the word of God but manipulate it. Like an eye for an eye, you kill someone, but in theory, killing is a sin.

I nod, my heart drumming wildly. "You think that they still do it? That the families that founded this place use it as a cover-up?"

He swipes his hair off his face again. "Maybe? There is the fact that the three sons of the families that founded this place are hound dogs who fuck selected girls that come through here. Their fathers aren't the faithful kind, if you know what I mean. None of them are. Some of the students here are part of their family's circle, whether it is business or alliance in some way. That can't be coincidence."

I let out a slow breath and raise my eyebrows. "Wow, Marc. That sounds—"

"Crazy?"

I nod and answer, "Yeah."

The door swings open and Jess comes in and I smile. "Hey."

She glances at Marc. "Hey. I see you found a friend," she says with a knowing smile.

"Marc, this is Jess, and Jess, this is Marc. He works in the library and was nice enough to show me around."

"Hi, Marc. It's nice meeting you. I'm sorry, but I came to whisk my roommate away to hang out at a party the swim team is heading to."

He glances at me and smiles. "I see. Well, it was nice meeting you, Gianna."

I'm holding the book in my hand, but I prefer to read it while I'm here, so I hold it out for him. "Look, I would like to leave this here and read it in between my shifts. Maybe you can tell me which chapter would be more interesting. You have told me so much about the history already."

He shifts uncomfortably and glances at Jess. "Okay, I can do that," he says, placing the book away in a particular spot. Can we exchange numbers?"

"Sure," I tell him, then rattle off my number. He enters it on his phone and sends me a quick text."

It chimes, but I don't open it, knowing it is just his number. I decide to save his contact information after I leave.

CHAPTER SIXTEEN

GIA

"HE SEEMS NICE. I love the way he calls you Gianna instead of Gia," Jess says.

We make it to our dorm, and she changes clothes while I stare at the too-small closet, wondering what I'm going to wear to this so-called party.

"Yeah, he seems nice." I glance at her. "Did you know Dravin, Reid, and Valen are known as the sons of Kenyan?"

Jess is applying makeup, sitting on her bed with her compact mirror open. "I heard about it from someone in class during my freshman year, but it's like no one dares to say it out loud. Like it's taboo or something, but yeah, I have heard that along with all the other shit that they do."

My interest is piqued by Marc mentioning the eye for an eye and that killing is a sin. What other things do they do? "Like, what other shit do they do?"

"Remember, Fuck girls, break their hearts. Fuck more girls, ruin their reputations, intimidate, deceive, and fuck people up when they want to and get away with it. Let's not forget the people that are in their so-called clique. Rich people. They also play the part of their little pets. I mean, they get away with everything."

"Did they really hurt you, Jess?"

I feel bad that people look at her weirdly when she is not looking. When I leave and she stays, I don't think it's because she is meeting someone. I think she is just watching and waiting. Like she is waiting for the ball to drop or something. I think what they did affected her more than she lets on.

She lowers her eyeliner pencil and compact mirror. The pained look on her face breaks something inside of me.

"Yeah, they posted pictures of me asleep with Garrett and the other girl but blurred out my face. Everyone knows it was me, though. They titled it "She plays both sides," and everyone whispers how I am so desperate that I will agree to be with anyone."

I shake my head. "Bastards. But why?"

Her shoulders rise and fall. "I don't know." Her voice cracks on the last part. She tries to wipe away a stray tear and pats her chick to avoid smudging her make-up.

'I'm so sorry, Jess."

"I almost left. I didn't want to come back. She laughs, but it's her way of calming herself and preventing her from breaking down into tears. It's like she is trying to hold herself together. Like a dam holding back all the tears from rushing forth. "Just, be careful. After seeing what Dravin did today, ignoring you and flirting in front of you after he asked you to come to the meet. I know he said you'd just be friends and he could screw around like he always does, but to ignore you when you were saying hello. Everyone saw it."

She looks at the flowers and the card Dravin sent me. "I don't want you to go through what I did. I don't want you to fall victim to their games." She lowers her voice. "I think it would be wise to just forget about them, Gia. I think you shouldn't take anything from Dravin or anyone in his circle."

I turn and look inside the closet. "So, who is going to be at this party?"

"The swim team from our school and all their followers, and I heard guys from Ohio State will be there. Why?"

I angle my head. "Let's hang out with Ohio State then. Why should we pay attention to Kenyan boys anyway? Fuck them and their stupid cliques."

Jess smiles. "I like it. What are you going to wear?"

———

We pull up to a house on the other side of town. It is big but nothing compared to Dravin and the houses on his street. This house is your regular upper-class type of residence.

"Whose place is this?" I ask Jess.

"One of the guys who got into Kenyan because his parents donated enough money to the university to build the pool center is Nick. He swims for Ohio State, though, but his parents love Kenyan. I guess to keep the peace every time we have a meeting, he throws a party at his house. I've only been here once before."

"Really?"

She closes the door to her car and locks it. "Yeah, it's where I met Reid for the first time."

"How did that go?"

"It went well. I walked in on him while he was screwing a girl on the sink in the bathroom."

"Classy."

"I know. It's what Reid does, classy shit."

We walk up the porch of the house. "You look great in the little black dress with the jacket. Pantyhose and Docs are a nice touch."

I look down. "Thanks, so do you."

Jess is wearing dangerously ripped jeans and a cropped fuzzy sweater. Although it is still warm enough to wear a dress, you still need a jacket when it's nightfall.

We walk in, and Nirvana is blaring through the speakers. People are drinking, smoking, and dancing. They all eye us curiously as we pass through. I silence my phone at Dravin's fourth text. After I threw away the card and roses, I decided not to answer him...ever.

I glance down at my phone while Jess is tugging me along.

> Dravin: I'm sorry about the swim meet.
>
> Dravin: Can we talk?
>
> Dravin: I said I was sorry.
>
> Dravin: Raven?

I then look at another text and it was the one Marc sent.

> Marc: I'm glad to have met you, Gianna. Don't end up hurt like your friend.

"Tell me about it," I mumble.

We reach the kitchen, and she hands me a sealed fruity wine cooler and I open the twist top and take a pull. The fruity concoction goes down my throat, chasing away the feelings and replacing them with reason. Do not fall for Dravin Bedford's shit or any of his so-called friends.

From the corner of my eye, I see a beer pong game being played and a crowd of people gathered around it. I can hear cheers and laughter when the crowd screams to chug it.

"Come on, Bedford, you can do better than that! You suck, just like Warren's sister. She sucked your dick after the meet and made the walk of shame." A guy with blonde shoulder-length hair says, laughing.

I lean against the corner of the wall and swallow the rest

of the wine cooler to calm the jealousy and anger radiating like an impending storm in my veins. How quickly he forgets that he invited me to cheer for him while he blatantly ignored me in front of everyone all for a blow job.

Jess stands next to me and watches the game. "What a shocker. Dick." Jess drawls sarcastically.

I walk over and grab another wine cooler, open the top, and tip it back to take another chug. Jess's eyes widen at how fast I'm drinking. "I think you might want to slow down on those. They can creep up on you."

"I can handle it."

She lifts a penciled eyebrow. "I know you're pissed, but that's the way he is, and there is nothing or no one that will change him. He doesn't know the meaning of friendship."

"Who are we talking about?" A deep voice says behind us.

I jump and when I look, I find myself getting lost in Dravin's gaze. He moves and grabs the wine cooler out of my grasp. I try to get it back from him, but he is so tall that he can hold it high in the air out of reach.

"Give it to me," I snap.

"No. You've had enough."

He takes the bottle and slides the tip in his mouth and sucks where my lips were seconds ago. He doesn't take a sip or a pull from it but simply sucks the tip of the bottle. His tongue slides over the circle of the rim. He sucks on his lips like he is savoring a hard candy.

It is the sexiest thing I have ever seen. It almost makes me forget how he treated me and what I heard he did with Warren's sister. Almost.

"What are you doing?"

"Saving you from drinking yourself stupid." He lowers his arm with the bottle and passes it to Valen, who tosses it in the trash. His lips lower to my ear. His cologne is probably called *Sinner* for how good it smells. "You wouldn't want to be tipsy or drunk around a guy like me, Raven. Friend or not, I wouldn't know how to stop if you told me you wanted me. I just tasted your sweet lips and I want more. I want to be the bottle you wrap that pretty mouth of yours around."

My head angles, and my cold, hard stare meets his, mine mixed with hurt and anger. "I think it's a little crowded and I don't like to share. It leaves a bad taste in my mouth. I'm sure you can ask Warren's sister, she's familiar with your flavor." I pull away and he flinches.

He didn't think I would find out. He must see the hurt in my eyes because he looks down, shielding his eyes from me. For one moment, I think he feels ashamed but then I think of the card he wrote and the flowers.

How quickly something ends before it even begins, even if it was a so-called friendship he was offering. If it was a lie, at least I was lucky enough to come out with my pride.

I step back, and he is still looking down, and his eyes slowly caress my body all the way until I see his face because I refuse to gaze into his eyes. "Find some other girl who falls for your shit. I've told you before, I'm not one of them. Kindly, fuck off."

I turn around to find Jess, but she is nowhere to be found. I decide I will call her from outside. I grab another wine cooler from the ice bucket and make my way outside.

CHAPTER SEVENTEEN

GIA

I MAKE it to the side of the house that is half-lit. There is no one around, so I quickly fish out my phone from my pocket to text Jess. The screen lights up, and I get a text.

> Dravin: Look up

My head whips up, and I look to my right. A sleek black sedan is waiting by the curb. Dravin is standing at the corner of the house, watching me. His jeans fit him like a cover model, hugging him in all the right places. He has on a black jacket, and his straight black hair shines even in the dark. He walks lithely over the grass that's crunching under his designer boots. The man can pull off the Gothic grudge look flawlessly.

He makes his way over to me. "Look at me," he demands.

I glare at him. My eyes must reflect the way I'm feeling.

"It's not what you think. Please, don't drink that." He points to the bottle. "Not out of anger or hurt because of something I have done. I never meant to hurt you, Raven. Come with me? I want to take you somewhere. Just you and me." He points to my phone. "Tell her you have a ride home. She is safe in there. No one will hurt her again, I promise."

"Why should I trust you? You are the last person I should trust. Especially with Jess."

He slides his hand through his hair, causing his bicep to flex. His build reminds me of Adam Peaty; all ripped but with more tattoos on his skin. He just got a blow job from that tramp and then he talks to me like I'm supposed to just forget her. I know I'm overreacting about the blow job thing. I shouldn't care. He offered friendship, and I agreed. He isn't my boyfriend or anything close, but the problem is that I wish he was boyfriend material. Maybe I just need to calm down and take him for what he is; it's nothing serious.

"It wasn't us that did that to your roommate. It was people she shouldn't have trusted. I had nothing to do with that, and it won't happen again."

"Why should I believe you?"

"I don't have anything to offer that would make you believe me other than my word. I would never tell you I could do something I couldn't. You just have to trust me."

I text Jess while he is standing there.

> Gia: Are you ok?

> Jess: Yes. I'm okay. I'm talking to Valen.

> Gia: I'm heading out. I will meet you at the dorm later. Text me when you leave and don't drink and drive.

> Jess: Valen barred me from the kitchen, only water.

I look up and find eyes clear as a blue sky and obsidian black watching me type in my phone. "Satisfied?" he asks.

I nod, and he waves his hand toward the car. A driver has the door open and is waiting for us to get in. What college student has a personal driver? How rich is Dravin Bedford? I must be tipsy, because I just agreed to take a ride with the devil.

He waits for me to slide in the back of the sedan. Black

leather touches the backs of my thighs, encased in black lace pantyhose. The privacy window is up, and my head turns to look at Dravin sliding inside the car.

A minute passes, and the car lunges forward. The tension inside the car begins to build and all of a sudden it feels hot. I slide my jacket off, and I'm left in the tiny black dress that has ridden up my thighs.

His eyes follow my movements inside the car and darken when they reach my thighs. Awareness creeps inside every nerve under my skin, yearning and wanting to touch and taste this man sitting beside me. I try to hide the reaction he causes in me with a single flick of his gaze or the way his beautiful eyes tell me things without him saying a word.

He makes me want to lay back and spread my body out as a sacrifice. I want to let him do whatever he wants, whenever he pleases.

The car has dark tinted windows that you can hardly see out of, especially at night. I'm trying to distract myself and figure out where we are when it suddenly stops.

The door is opened, and I see that we are in front of his house.

"What are we doing here?"

He knows what I really want to ask is why did you bring me to your house?

"I want to spend time getting to know you. Preferably, alone."

I exit out of the car and follow him up the walkway. He opens the door electronically with his thumbprint on a black screen I never noticed was there. Impressive. We walk in, and the first thing I notice is that he pulls out his phone and changes the color of the pool from red to deep blue.

"I think you prefer it to be this color?"

How did he know that? I guess I'm not good at hiding my expressions when I don't like something. Or maybe he sees my thoughts in my eyes the same way I feel like I can read his sometimes.

My eyes find his. "How did you know?"

"I pay attention to a lot of things."

He takes my jacket and places it on the island, then grabs my hand and leads me outside. "What are we doing out here?"

He ignores my question and takes his jacket off and lifts his shirt over his head and I suck in a breath at the ripple of muscle as he moves his arms. His chest is bare except for the hard lines of his muscles and ink swirling in different shades and colors. His jeans come off next, and he is left in his snug-fitting black boxers that don't leave much to the imagination.

The temperature has dropped, but he doesn't shiver. It is like he is used to the cold being out here next to the pool.

We stand staring at each other. I'm memorizing every inch of his chiseled body while he stands there, allowing me to get my fill. He doesn't smirk or give me any indication that I'm inflating his ego. He just silently lets me admire him. I want to touch him and feel his skin beneath my fingers. He is so... complicated. He has an achingly beautiful darkness, but under all that darkness is a pain. An unbearable pain that I can tell he is trying to shed from somewhere so deep, it is almost haunting.

His hands reach out and touch the hollow space on my neck. His thumb slides gently like a soft rose against my skin feeling the rapid beat of my pulse. My head tilts so I can see his wrist, and I see tiny scars that he most likely inflicted on himself. They are hidden underneath his wrist tattoos, but I see them.

My lips reach his wrist. I close my eyes and place a kiss to where the faint scars are shining under the single yellow light illuminating us in the backyard. I bear witness to the scars of his pain. They are long and vertical but deep enough that it must have hurt.

"That must have hurt," I whisper, a tear escaping the corner of my eye and falling down my cheek.

"I'm so sorry."

He cups my cheek with his open palm and wipes my tears with his thumb. He doesn't respond, but his actions are enough to tell me that Dravin is haunted by a deep pain. A loss so profound that it scares me because it makes me question everything I have heard about him. When Dravin is alone with me, I see a side of him so opposite of the man everyone talks about at school.

My eyes blur when I open them and find his own reflected at me like a mirror. He leans down and slowly pulls my dress up over my head. I'm left in only my bra, panties, pantyhose, and Docs. He kneels and removes my shoes. He tilts his head up silently, asking for permission before sliding my pantyhose off, leaving me in my black bra and lace panties.

I don't know why I let him bring me here and why I'm practically naked alone in his house by the pool. But I do know that I want to be here. I want to be near him. He's a mystery that calls to me. A mystery I want to unravel.

He grips my wrist and leads me to the sundeck at the edge of the pool. The water is glowing deep blue, and I expect it to be cold, but when my foot feels the water, it is warm like the water from a cozy bath—not too hot but not cold enough to cause me to shiver.

My body is tingling in anticipation when he entwines his fingers through mine. When we finally are at the edge, he slides in without releasing my hand. The water is at his waist, and I sit at the edge of the pool's sun deck until the water just covers my panties. He nudges my legs apart and he glides forward so my thighs are around his hips.

His forehead rests between my breasts and I slide my fingers through his dark hair.

"I want to kiss you right now, Raven. But I don't want you to think I brought you here to take advantage of you. I just wanted to share with you where I'm at peace. The water is where I feel like I'm at home. It has been my favorite place ever since I was five. My mother was afraid I would drown, so she hired a swimming instructor to teach me how to swim. It was the first time I felt alive. Truly alive. I was at peace. I swam every day after that. My mother made sure I had an indoor pool where I could swim year-round."

He raises his head and I look at him. "I love poetry. My parents were this happy couple when I was a kid, and I loved the idea of falling in love. Except when they divorced, I learned it was all a lie. I was so heartbroken that my dad cheated on my mother, and she filed for divorce. I stopped writing after that. My mother was a devoted Catholic who brought me to church every Sunday, even if I didn't want to go. I had this grand idea of love and what it was supposed to be like. Because of that idea, I would write. The words would come pouring out of me.

It was like I could speak to the dead by expressing my innermost feelings. If I were in love or sad. All my thoughts could be paired down into a single sentence or maybe three; it didn't matter. What mattered was that somewhere, someday, someone would read them. Even if I were dead, I believed that others would be able to see it no matter what. Like the bible was written for people who believed in the word of God on Earth, it was written so people could hear his message, but I wanted my own message to be heard."

"Do you believe in God?" he asks quietly.

"I believe in faith. I believe you have to have faith in something."

"Do you?"

"No. I don't."

"How about love?

He shakes his head. "I was taught love is a weakness. It makes you vulnerable, and that is when you lose." He raises his head and places his hands on the edge of the deck beside my outer thighs. "I don't like to lose."

I lean back, holding myself with the palms of my hands facing down on the concrete of the sundeck. The water reaches above my wrists, and I can feel the tips of my hair getting wet as I lean back. "Have you ever been in love?" I ask him.

He shakes his head. "Have you?"

"No," I say.

I'm being honest with him. This is a side of Dravin I would have never thought to see. I know deep inside, this is the side I prefer. The one I can see for myself and not what people tell me I should expect. They say he is dangerous and tell me I should steer clear, but I have yet to see what they mean about him being dangerous; the only danger he could be is to my heart. I can see he is mysterious and private. One thing I have noticed, though, is that no one stops him. He does what he wants, when he wants.

"Good, otherwise you're no use to me."

What? What does he mean by that?

Before I can ask him, he pushes back, creating a wave in the pool and the sound of water soothing me as he begins to swim laps. I can see his muscles moving underwater against the glow of the pool. I didn't get to see him swim earlier, and I have to say that Dravin's swimming is pure perfection. Every stroke of his arms is perfect, like blades cutting through the water. He makes it back, flips under, and pushes off again five more times. When he finally stops, I notice one thing. He isn't even out of breath.

He comes up out of the water and reaches out his hand so I can take it. I slide my hand in his and he smoothly lifts me so I can stand.

He tugs me gently so I am close enough to admire the way the drops of water slide down his hard muscles like water falling over hard glass. I shiver against the cold because the bottom half of me is wet, and the tips of my hair are causing the tiny hairs on my back to stand. He hands me a towel from the towel warmer, and I am instantly enveloped in warmth.

Trying to break the awkward silence, I ask, "What do you do during the winter when it's snowing? How do you swim?"

He turns his head while he is drying himself. "I practice on campus. It is open year-round, and they heat the pool during winter."

I wonder why he wants to live alone. I know Reid moved in with him, but I have the feeling that it was Reid's choice and not Dravin's. I can't help myself. I want to know more about him.

"Why do you live alone? I see that you are mostly alone all the time."

"I don't have many friends and prefer to keep the ones I trust close."

"You mean Reid and Valen?"

He nods. "I have known them almost my whole life. They are the only people I trust." He turns around when we get to the foot of the stairs. I pause, keeping the huge towel wrapped around my body, and subconsciously realize I left my clothes outside when I followed him. "If you ever find that I'm not around, you can trust them. They won't hurt you."

Why would anyone try to hurt me? What he is saying doesn't make sense. I haven't done anything to anyone. He turns around and begins to climb the stairs, but I stay and don't follow. I'm not sure I want to follow or what it would mean if I did. I'm wrapped in a warm towel with only my panties and bra.

When he senses that I'm not following, he stops but doesn't turn around, as if it is costing him the opportunity to say his next words. It is as if he is uncertain if what is going to happen next is the right choice.

I decide for him. "I need to go get my clothes and I will be on my way."

He bows his head. "You don't need them, Raven. I promise to not do anything you don't want me to. I want you to stay. I *need* you to stay."

I bite my lip, not knowing if this is the right move. One voice in my head is telling me I should run. Then another voice is telling me to succumb. Resisting him is futile. I know I will give him what he wants, even if what he wants right now is me. There is nothing anyone can do to stop him. He is everywhere. There is no escaping him, and I would be lying if I told myself I didn't want to stay and find out what it was like to be with him. He has a magmatism that draws you in, like right now, as I place one foot on the steps and then the next sealing my fate. Deep down, I know that after tonight, I will never be the same. There is no one like him. I will want him for the rest of my life, even if I can only have a tiny piece of him. A little piece of Dravin is better than having nothing at all.

CHAPTER EIGHTEEN

GIA

I FOLLOW him into his room and see the massive bed. Its carved bed frame with intricate swirls looks like it's a table of sacrifice for the pleasures that will take place. My thighs clench and wetness pools between my legs and it's not because I was sitting in a pool.

Once I'm inside, he closes the door and locks it. His eyes find mine, but he stays silent. I'm standing still as a statue, gripping the towel like it's going to save me from whatever he has planned. He moves to the left of his enormous room. There are two double doors he opens that lead to a bathroom with a massive tub and a shower. The entire room is a black marble with swirls of grey-like veins over the glossy surface.

The accents are shiny gold with glass that encases the shower. My eyes find the black free-standing porcelain bathtub, and I notice it has never been used. The plastic is still on the knobs from when it was installed.

"You've never used it?"

He knows I mean the bathtub seeing as I'm standing right next to it, fascinated by the beautiful knobs and accented white rocks underneath.

He shakes his head. "No," he answers curtly, like the topic is not up for discussion. His eyes darken with pain as he looks at me standing next to it. I want to know more about that look, but I'm afraid to ask.

He motions for me to walk closer to the shower then presses buttons on an electronic screen and the water shoots out like rain from the ceiling. When I walk closer, I notice one wall is all rocks and water is cascading down like a waterfall.

"This is gorgeous."

It really is. I never thought a bathroom could be so enchanting. Just seeing it is an experience.

He opens the glass door and walks over and tugs my hand so it will slip and release the towel. It falls in a heap on the floor at my feet between us. His eyes slowly scroll over my body. My nipples harden under my black bra and my heart beats so loudly I'm sure he can hear it. I have never been naked in front of a man before.

My lips part and my eyes close. I feel the steam coming out of the hot shower all around me and the sound of water hitting the marble like rain.

"Dravin," I whisper.

"Yes, Raven."

My eyes are still closed because I can't believe I'm here, half-naked, alone with him in his bathroom. "Why do you want me to stay with you?"

"I told you. I need you, and I know deep down you need me, too."

He slides the straps of my bra down one shoulder then the next. My nipples are on the edge of the thin fabric as I keep my eyes closed. I know if I open them, I will see in his eyes what he is feeling, and it terrifies me because I don't know if I can handle it. I don't want to run. I want to feel.

I can feel his fingers on my back, and with expert deftness, he releases the clasp of my bra. It falls to the floor like a ribbon that has been cut. He steps closer and I feel the tingle of his breath as he slides his fingers under the band of my panties, over my hips, and down my thighs. I finally open my eyes and fling them with my foot to the side.

I'm naked as the day I was born, thankful I decided to shave everything before the party. His eyes travel over every part of me. When they land on mine, I look to the left and see our reflection in the mirror fogged with steam.

In one swoop, he removes his boxers, and his massive hard cock is bobbing between us. I glance down and he smirks since I can see his other two piercings on the head. The tip glistens with precum, and my eyes travel above, noticing he shaves… everywhere.

He reaches out his hand, linking it with mine, and walks us over to the shower until we are under the spray. My eyes blink as the water falls over us like we are in the middle of a storm. A storm we are creating that will be brutal and beautiful all at the same time. I feel it. Already…right now. I know I could love him. But we both know that he cannot love. It is in his eyes, a darkness that forbids it. He's stunning and terrifying, and I want to experience every part of him, even if he breaks me.

He places body wash in his hands and slowly slides his fingers over my skin. I can feel his hands burning my flesh leaving ashes in its wake. I will never forget this moment, his touch, and the way he is memorizing the feel of my skin and every curve of my body.

His eyes caress my face while his hands caress my skin. "Your skin is so soft," he says. But I knew it would be. Just like I knew you would be this beautiful, this pure."

My body responds by allowing him to wash me everywhere. His fingers touch every part of my body, and it's like he is touching every part of my soul. No other man has touched me like this, and I'll always remember the feeling—the feeling of falling in love for the first time.

He doesn't say much, but the few words that escape his lips hold so much meaning. It is a gift for me to have his attention when his words are this beautiful, because words are his gift.

When he is done with my body, he lathers shampoo in my hair, and I almost gasp from the pleasure. It feels so intimate. I never thought a man could make love to a woman just with his hands. He rinses the soap from my dark strands, and I take his soap and rub my hands over the hardness of his muscles.

I glide my fingers over the lines of the ink on his skin and he watches me. The water sliding down his straight black hair like a river over his chest muscles. My nipples are achingly close to his torso and my cheeks smolder when my hand dips low near his cock.

It hardens in response to my fingers near its length. His hands guide mine and the smooth velvet under my fingers brings a whimper from my throat. His cock is hard, thick, and long. It's beautiful.

"You are gorgeous," I blurt.

He grins and tilts his head like he is studying me while I touch him. I stroke his length and a hiss escapes his lips.

"If you keep doing that, beautiful, I won't last much longer."

I stop and release him, embarrassment flooding me. I bite my lip and peer up. I was caught up in the fascination of his body, not thinking that I was actually jerking him off.

My eyes lower in embarrassment but he lifts my chin with his finger. He leans close and blocks the spray of water. My eyes lift, and it's like the storm that was brewing within him breaks loose, and he takes my lips in a scorching hot kiss. A gasp tears from my throat and my spine tingles like electricity surging through me straight to the area between my legs. My hands slide up his neck until they are wrapped around him, and I press my body as close as I can to his, hoping we can stay fused together.

He lifts me and holds me gently against the marble. I'm so lost in the scent of him as his tongue explores my mouth. I swear I can hear a low growl escape his throat. It's like he's the predator, and he has finally found his Prey.

Our mouths battle the storm of our tongues, our mingled breaths, in a delicious harmony. I have never had a kiss so powerful and all consuming. Nothing can compare to what I feel when I'm with Dravin.

Dravin's touch and kiss is not like a hot sex scene from an erotica novel. Pure lust and all-consuming need. It's different. It's consuming. It's possessive. His warm tongue slowly slides up from the base of my neck, until his lips meet mine again. I suck his top lip and then his bottom like I can't get enough of him. I can still taste him when we finally pull away to breathe.

He sets me back down on the floor and slides his hand over my thigh and lifts my leg over his hip. His fingers find the slit between the folds of my pussy and I whimper. His fingers find my clit and he softly rubs me.

"Oh my God," I say breathlessly.

"I'll be anything you want, Raven." He gently slides his finger inside, and I arch my back. "Is this okay? If you want me to stop, I will. I'll never hurt you."

My heart melts at his words, and I whisper, "It's ok. I want you, Dravin."

His mouth is at that curve of my neck. "That's what I'm afraid of," he rasps.

Before I can think about the meaning of his words, he begins his assault.

I moan when he slips a finger inside me and rubs my clit with his thumb in a delicious rhythm making my climax build and my nipples harden. He lowers his head and takes my nipple between his lips. My body responds, and I arch my back, but he holds me in place. I'm at his mercy while he slides his fingers in and out.

"You're so tight, baby. I can feel you squeezing my fingers. Look at me," he rasps.

Our eyes meet, and what I see is a beautiful storm—a battle between good and bad, light and dark. It's just like before, except this time, it's all for me. I don't know how he can make me feel safe and frightened all at once. It is like he is two distinctive people wrapped in one.

"You make me feel so good, Dravin. Don't stop," I plead.

He keeps sliding his fingers in and out and I know I'm not going to last. I want him to keep touching me like this forever. He doesn't relent and I shutter.

He growls in his throat. "Come, my Raven. Let me see how you break for me."

His name escapes my lips in a breathless whisper as I come. "Dravin."

CHAPTER NINETEEN

GIA

THE LIGHT FILTERS in through the window, waking me from my sleep. My eyes open, and I squint at the bright light coming from the sun. For a minute, I thought last night was a dream but when my eyes regain their focus, it all comes back. The pool, the shower, and the way Dravin kissed me when he made me come on his fingers.

My hand reaches out, and I notice his side is empty. The satin sheets are cold and when I lift my head, I see that I'm in Dravin's room, alone.

"It wasn't a dream," I mumble.

My eyes find the wall with the paintings I hate so much, and I'm shocked to find them missing. Odd. Why would he take them down?

My head turns and I notice there is a note and a single black rose on the pillow.

I lift the rose and close my eyes to smell the flowery scent.

> *I refuse to exhale. Not until I have your dreams and the taste of your breath on my lips.*
> *Dravin*

I reread the words, and my heart sings even though I'm scared. I'm scared because I'm in love with a dark, broken man—a gorgeous man who has captured my soul with every glance of his beautiful eyes.

I raise the sheet from the bed, and I notice I'm naked underneath. I look around and don't see my clothes, but I see a black box with a red ribbon at the foot of the bed.

I crawl over on my hands and knees, careful to keep the satin sheet over my breasts in case the door opens.

It reads, *"It's for you, Open it."*

I smile, untie the ribbon, and open the lid of the oversized box. I gasp when I see a complete Phillip Plein outfit. It looks like the dress I wore last night, except it is an expensive version made of gorgeous, soft fabric. I look down and notice there are boots to match.

I grab the box and head into the bathroom, where I see something dangling from my throat. I lean closer to the mirror and see it is a black ribbon choker necklace with a Raven adorned with black diamonds.

I stare at the girl in the mirror, and I smile. It isn't like me to accept such lavish gifts, but I want to feel like this is real and that Dravin is mine and I am his.

I want to know what it feels like to be in love with someone like him. He was honest last night in telling me he sees love as a weakness, and maybe he is right, but this feels right. At least, to me, it does. I can have enough love for us both until he gives in to his feelings or decides to get rid of me.

I wash up and find a new toothbrush. "He thinks of everything," I mutter.

I wonder how many girls he brings home and does the same things for. How many girls have been standing here in this very bathroom wondering the same thing? I realize I'm one of them, but the only difference is, I know I'm temporary. I have no hopes for it to ever be more than what it is. Well, I do have hopes, but I'm trying very hard to be realistic. I'm trying to guard my heart. This infatuation that will probably end up in vexation.

———

I make my way down the stairs and hear voices from the kitchen.

"I don't know who he has up there. He never brings girls to his room," Valen whispers.

I listen and smile to myself at the words every girl wants to hear. I am the only girl who got to spend the night with Dravin in his room, which made my initial thought in the bathroom regarding all the girls before me all wrong. No one has seen the side of Dravin that I got to experience last night and this morning.

My footsteps make a sound on the steps and both Reid and Valen look over with smirks on their faces.

"Now we know who he has holed up there," Valen says.

He quickly fixes me a plate with eggs and bacon and places it in front of the stool. "Here you are, milady," he says with a smile.

"Thank you."

"My pleasure. I'm glad I made extra."

Reid slaps him upside the head. "You made extra in hopes of seeing who he had up there."

I put my hand over my mouth to keep myself from laughing. "It's all good, thanks anyway."

I look around, searching for any sign of Dravin, but I see that we are the only three in the kitchen. I'm about to open my mouth.

"He left," Reid says. He gives me a sorry expression.

I shrug my shoulder because I expected Dravin to do the

disappearing act in the morning. The good news is that I haven't slept with him in the true sense. I still have that if he disappears on my already.

"Don't look at me like that," I tell Reid. "I'm not doing the walk of shame."

Valen laughs. "Yeah, right. Are you telling me right now that you didn't have sex last night with the infamous Dravin Bedford?"

"If you are asking if I rode his cock the answer is no."

Valen shakes his head and Reid looks at me like I'm a dragon with three heads.

"You are telling us he let you sleep in his bed and stay the night and he didn't smash?"

"Is that hard to believe?" I ask.

"This is Dravin. I'm surprised you're in this house." He points his finger up and down. "Nice clothes, by the way."

I peer down and smooth the dress. "I know," I say, stepping down the remaining stairs, taking a seat, and digging the fork in the eggs. "I didn't buy them. He did."

They both raise their brows and lean on the marble island and watch me eat. They both keep staring at me. After a few seconds, I put the fork down.

"What?"

Reid is the first to answer. "Do you have a magical pussy?"

I snicker. "No."

"She does," Valen teases. "She really does. I'm mad now."

"Why?"

His tone gets serious, and I see his demeanor change. I lean back on the stool. I look at Reid, and he seems unaffected by Valen's serious expression.

Valen's eyes turn dark. A darkness I have never seen, and he tilts his head. "I would have loved to have a taste."

My head whips to Reid, but he says nothing. Dravin told me I could trust them when he wasn't here but now, I'm not so sure. The hair on the back of my neck rises, and my appetite suddenly vanishes. Valen just went from zero to creepy in one second flat. What. The. Fuck?

My hands begin to shake nervously as I slide my hair behind my ear. "I-I think I need to get going. Jess must be worried sick about me."

"She's still in bed," Reid deadpans.

"What?"

Reid looks up toward the second floor and then back at me with a knowing smile. "Garret is a distant memory."

Valen licks his lips, and the message is clear. They fucked Jess last night. They. As in, both of them.

Damn it, Jess.

My worried expression tells them I'm not happy about it. Jess is my roommate, and I can safely say my friend—not my best friend, but my friend.

"It's ok, Gia. We were gentle," Valen says.

"Fuck you. Both of you," I snap.

"If Dravin allows it, that can always be arranged. We love new pussy," Valen drawls.

"Chill, Valen," Reid warns.

I rip my eyes from Valen and realize that he is just playing around.

I slide off the stool and look for my jacket that has my phone and wallet. "He didn't mean it," Reid says, walking after me.

"I'm sorry, Gia. I was messing around. Jess is sleeping upstairs if you want to go wake her. I pause because if I leave, that will mean I leave her with these two assholes. I don't know how she feels about them or if she is really ok.

"Relax, Gia. She's ok. I would never let anything happen to her," Reid says quietly.

I raise my chin. "I need to see her."

He turns around and leads me to the stairs. I glare at Valen, wiping the smirk from his face, and raise my middle finger.

"Anytime, baby."

"Quit it, Valen. Dravin is going to kick your ass for upsetting her."

"Whatever," he mutters.

"Valen doesn't take anything seriously. You will get used to his moods."

"I have a feeling I won't," I quip.

He stops in front of his door and angles his head like he is talking to the wood floor. "She's tired. We had her up all night."

I hold my breath when he opens the door. Jess is sprawled on her back, with the sheet covering only her breasts and the apex of her thighs. She must sense that someone is in the room because she stretches and rises on her elbows.

Her eyes focus on Reid, and when she sees me, they widen. She looks down and licks her lips. Her eyes lock on Reid standing in front of me, but I can't see his expression.

"Hey," she says to me.

"Get dressed. She's waiting for you to leave," he says dryly.

Asshole. He just slept with her and is dismissing her like she is a piece of meat left on a plate he doesn't want to eat anymore.

"Come on. Let's go. Our time is up here."

She nods and grips the sheet tighter, avoiding looking at Reid. My stomach clenches for her. I feel sorry for Jess. He simply dismissed her like she was nothing. Dravin's disappearance isn't any better. He just left a note and gift as an excuse for his absence, but he didn't promise me anything, and I was willing to participate the whole night. I shouldn't feel a tang bit disappointed, but I do.

CHAPTER TWENTY

GIA

I MAKE my way out of the library and Marc gives me a smile as he walks out the opposite door toward his class.

"Hey, how was your weekend? Are you ready for poetry today?"

We didn't discuss what happened after Jess and I made it home yesterday. We were easily persuaded to hang out with the dubbed sons of Kenyan. I was with one, and she was with the other two. How they managed to steer the night into having us to themselves is a wonder all in itself.

We went about our business, finishing schoolwork, doing laundry, and even going to pick up something to eat at the café. The topic of them was never brought up. It was like it never happened.

"It was good, how was yours?

He gives me a grin. "I visited my parents and had dinner."

I instantly feel a pang of longing. I remember when my parents were together and we would have Sunday brunch together, but come to think of it, the last three years, I remember a strained feeling at the table. I also remember my father excusing himself to go to the bathroom—a lot. Now I know it was because he was seeing someone else behind my mother's back. All the signs were there, but my mother and I never picked up on them.

"That must have been really nice."

"Maybe, you could—"

A large shadow comes up from the corner of my eye. "No. She can't." Dravin's voice says in an icy tone.

Marc's eyes widen with a stricken look on his face. He looks from me to Dravin.

"Hi," I squeak.

My eyes travel over his black jacket and stonewashed denim jeans. All I can think about is his mouth-watering hard chest. I remember rubbing soap over his skin and watching it glide off with the spray of water.

I must be ogling him because he gives me a grin and says, "Eyes up here, beautiful."

My cheeks flush at being caught red-handed, and my eyes meet his stormy ones. One minute, they are annoyed; the next, they are calm and collected.

I don't know what to say, but I have recovered from embarrassing myself further. I wave my hand at Marc. "Marc, this is Dravin. Dr—"

Marc interrupts me, "I know. Everyone knows who he is, Gianna."

Marc sounds irritated, but I don't know why. His boyish charm vanished the moment Dravin showed up.

"I'm gonna get to class," I tell them.

I don't have time for guys who treat me like crap. One disappears after a night with me and the other gives me attitude when all I was doing was trying to be nice. I get that Dravin was a tad rude answering for me, but Marc didn't have to take it out on me.

"I'll walk you," Dravin says in a clipped tone.

Marc steps back and looks at Dravin with disdain. He clearly doesn't like him.

"I would be careful if I were you," Dravin warns Marc.

"Consider yourself warned."

"Why?" I ask, clearly annoyed.

He passes by Marc while they size each other up. Dravin is more muscular, but they are both the same height. "Because he wants to fuck you. He just has a different approach."

My eyes widen and Marc's lip curls. "She isn't some plaything."

Marc's eyes seek me out. "He's going to hurt you, Gianna. He and his little clique do it to all the girls who come through here, who don't know what they're about. It's all a game to them. You and every girl that—"

Dravin suddenly grabs him by the throat and slams Marc against the wall. "Keep running your mouth, and you will see what happens," Dravin growls.

Marc grips Dravin's hand that is wrapped around his throat, trying to gasp for air.

"Dravin! Let him go," I demand.

People walking by look over but don't stop. It's like they know better than to interfere. When I see one of the faces of passersby, all I see is fear. They are afraid of Dravin.

"Dravin, please."

He releases him, and Marc gasps for air in a coughing fit. "You choked me, you fucking psycho. You need to go back to that shrink of yours."

Shrink? Dravin has a mental problem? I mean, besides his solitude, the weird pictures he took down in his room, the hot and cold, and the temper. I could safely say he is a little off but psycho. He wouldn't be on the swim team or in this school. *He has money, and money gets you a free pass.*

Dravin walks back and shoves him. "I'll deal with you later." He grabs me by the arm, and I shrug him off.

"You can't just attack people because they say things

about you. What is wrong with you? You could have really hurt him."

"Don't listen to everything you hear."

I place my hands on my hips under my oversized knitted sweater. "Why? Because it's closer to the truth?"

"Because listening to other people can get you thinking the wrong shit, and the next thing you know, you're taking the wrong side."

"His side is the wrong side, and yours isn't. Why do I have to pick a side? I'm on my side."

"So am I. Let's go."

He walks toward my class, and when we get there, I walk through the door and notice he follows me inside. I take a seat and he sits in the one right above me."

I look up. He thumbs his nose piercing, and his eyes widen sarcastically. "What?"

"What are you doing? "

"What does it look like? I'm sitting in class."

A group of girls walk in, and they notice him. One gives him a wink, and the other three give him knowing smiles. He tilts his head and looks at me and then at the blonde.

I turn around, rolling my eyes. "Let me guess, they're not scholarship students and they don't live in the dorms."

He leans forward. "You're catching on."

Something dawns on me. I think about Marc and what he said. When he walks into the class a few moments later, his neck is red from where Dravin almost choked the life out of him. His accusations repeatedly play in my head, and I remember what Jess said. The limited number of people in the dorms. How she told me certain people are part of Dravin, Reid, and Valen's group. Why are the less fortunate exploited

and people like Veronica aren't? It is like two sides, the preda-
tors and the...Prey.

The professor walks in and smiles at everyone, but when
his eyes land on mine, he has this strange look. It's the same
look Valen had when he—

Wait, wait. I am missing something, or I'm missing
nothing at all. It is all right here. I look around and pick out
the rich guys, who all give me side glances. They look at me
like Valen did the day after my night with Dravin. Dravin
looked at me the same way when he tried to come on to me in
the bathroom—and the cemetery.

I turn my head, and the chessboard pieces begin to fall in
place. Suddenly, I realize that I'm one of them.

I'm a pawn.

I'm one of the...Prey.

Dravin's words out in the hallway, right before walking in,
are coming back to me on repeat. *He wants to fuck you. He
just has a different approach.*

Valen's words in the kitchen and Reid's talk about Jess
being in bed after sleeping with both of them. Then everything comes full circle, or maybe semi-circle. Oh, My. God. I
close my eyes. My only answer to the thoughts in my head
is...why?

A voice is saying something, yet I can't make it out.

"Miss Taylor. Miss Taylor?"

I shake my head, snapping my mind out of its funk. My
eyes find Professor Whitmore looking at me, and I notice the
blank stares aimed at me from everyone around the room.

"Yes," I croak.

"I'm glad to have gotten your attention. I was making sure
you were present in my class. I—"

He glances behind me and stops mid-sentence. I have the feeling the look Dravin is giving him must be the reason. The guy has the power to silence people with a single glance. The professor's face strangely looks like a cross between surprise and fear.

The professor's eyes land on me once again. "I'm sorry. I was just trying to make sure you were with us."

I sink further in my chair. This is college, not high school. How much power does Dravin have that even the professors get tongue-tied? Normally, in a prestigious school like this, no one can sway a professor. It is their class, and they conduct it based on the rules the college sets forth, but apparently, those rules don't apply—at least, not with Dravin present.

The class moved along, and the only thing I was assigned was a journal, where we had to write a few lines of poetry to get familiar with prose. Basically, we put what we felt on paper, and he will randomly select someone to read and discuss it. Then, I will study the works of other great poets, my favorite being Edward Allen Poe.

CHAPTER TWENTY ONE

DRAVIN

I'M CLOSING my poetry journal when my phone rings on my desk in my room. I look at the screen, and Veronica's name flashes at me like a warning beacon.

I take a deep breath and answer the phone. "What?"

"I see you're taking this bet a little bit too personally. Not that I'm complaining, but I'm shocked at how long it's taking you to break her."

"There wasn't a time limit, and he isn't fucking her, so you should be happy. Let it go. You got what you wanted."

She sighs. The breath making a horrible wind noise through the phone. "So far. Except he isn't paying attention to me and still thinks he has a chance. You are moving too slow for my taste. One would think you are wooing her or something. You're not catching feelings for her, are you?"

"What makes you say that?" I ask, leaning in my chair.

"I don't know. Maybe it's the fact that you are temperamental when it comes to her—protective even. I don't think I didn't hear about your explosive rage on poor Marc in the hallway."

"What about it?"

She laughs like a villain in a Disney movie. "Oh, come now. It's obvious, Dravin. You're afraid to lose and even more afraid someone else might beat you to her."

"Leave it alone, Veronica."

"I think I won't." I can hear her pout over the phone.

It is just like Veronica to take things up a notch. She can't stand someone else getting attention. If her father wasn't who he was, I would have eliminated her a long time ago. Not only is she unstable, but her penchant for vengeance is a liability only her father overlooks.

"I think you need to rethink your intentions concerning Gia."

"Are you threatening me?"

"Maybe," I answer.

"I don't do well with threats. I thought you wanted me, Dravin. Did she change your mind when she showed you her tight pootie?"

"Jealous."

"As if. I'm not jealous. I could have fucked you a long, long time ago. It would be a shame though for her to find out she is just a game. A little pawn in a game in which she means nothing to you. You'll fuck her and get me in the process."

"Fuck you, Veronica."

She's trying to get to me through Gia, and I'm afraid she probably can.

She chuckles. "Oh, don't worry, Dravin. I'm planning on it."

Anger takes over, and I growl, "Leave her alone, Veronica."

"Oh, I'm so scared. What will your father think when he finds out you're threatening me over a low-class broke piece of ass? Are you afraid you finally met the one girl who can bring the infamous Dravin Bedford to his knees? I'm going to enjoy watching when she finally realizes that everything is all a lie and that she is just another pawn in the little games we all play with the less fortunate."

I hang up before I throw my cell phone across the room. "Stupid cunt," I mumble.

I should have told her to fuck off when she came to me, but now things have changed. This isn't about a bet anymore. I don't think this was ever about Warren and him dismissing her. She wants to break Gianna because of the attention she has and the fact that she can make me lose all sense of purpose when I'm around her. I have never lost because of a girl. But Gianna is different; she is gorgeous and has a body that was created with care and purpose. Her purpose is to make every man lose his mind if he is allowed the gift of glancing underneath her clothes. I got that glance, and here I am, losing my mind. Her innocence draws me to her. She won't drop to her knees for a man. She makes him fall to his knees first and beg. The taste of her is addicting. She is fast becoming an addiction of mine. I tasted her mouth, and now I want all of her.

I have never had to wait to have sex with a girl. I have never had to try. I could have taken it further in the shower, but something told me she would have stopped if it got too far, and I didn't want our first time to be in the bathroom. I know she is into me, but I also know she feels that it would mean nothing. She has no idea how wrong she is. It doesn't matter how many diamonds, custom necklaces, clothes, or black roses I buy her, it's not the way to get her. I want her body, but I also want more. I want all of her. I'm just afraid I'm going to break her in the process.

My eyes close and one of my last conversations with my mother comes back to me. A memory that I have savored since her tragic passing. It was the beginning of my junior year in high school after she found my father screwing the maid in their bedroom. My father taught me that love was a weakness that should never be a factor in my life. He said that he wasn't cheating on my mother and that she knew the terms of their marriage. He could screw whoever he wanted, and she could do the same. But my mother never did. She fell in love with my father, and the pain I saw her in broke me every day. It made me realize that my father was right when it came to love. It was a weakness that cost my mother her life. I just wondered what made her do it. What pushed her over the edge?

"You will meet a girl one day, Dravin. She will be different than all the others. Whole and pure-hearted. She will come to you like a Raven. It will all make sense when you meet her. She will call to you like no other. Protect her, and she will guide you. She will teach you things I cannot and your father is incapable of. Everything will make sense to you. What the meaning of life is. There will be only one like her. When you feel lost, she will be there. Don't ever take her for granted, and you must protect her because if anyone finds out that she means more to you than all the others, they will destroy her or, worse, take her away from you. Always remember, she is not like the others.

"How do you know all of this?" I ask.

"Because it happened to me, and I didn't listen. I took him for granted. I tried to love your father, but he deceived me, and I don't want it to happen to you, Dravin. Follow the order, but don't let it turn you into something that makes you a monster."

"Okay, mom. I promise."

"I will always love you, Dravin."

"I love you too, mom. Always."

CHAPTER TWENTY TWO

GIA

"YES, Mom. I promise to go to church."

I roll my eyes. My mother always makes sure I go to church. I find it boring, but I respect the word of God. Most of the time. I was kind of upset at him because everything I believed in with my parents was a lie. You would think that people who attend church for quite some time and preach the word of God wouldn't be liars. I'm more of a see-it-to-believe-it kind of girl.

In the end, all I have seen is lies. Some of the biggest sinners are inside the church, not out of it. It is like they are trying to cover up their sins by attending. I find that just because a person attends church, doesn't mean they are more holy than those who don't attend church. On the contrary, they can be just as evil.

"Are you coming home for Thanksgiving?"

She means to her apartment. That is all she could afford after she divorced my father. My father stayed in Wisconsin and decided to buy a nice big house with his younger girl-friend. I mean, she is only seven years older than me, making her twenty-eight to my father's forty-five.

"I have to go to dads. I told you this."

"I know. He told me I could join you, but I think it would be rather awkward for me to be there with him and...her."

I know she is referring to Stephanie, my father's girlfriend, aka Side Piece, who has now become the official girlfriend.

"I know this is hard, Mom, but—"

"Are you bringing anyone? Have you met someone?"

I shake my head even though I know she can't see me. "No—I mean yes. I—"

"Which is it? Yes or no?"

"I don't know mom. It's complicated."

"Well, if he can't see how amazing you are, then he isn't worth your time. Does he go to church?"

I have had enough. "Mom, I have to go."

I hang up, instantly regretting hanging up on her, and take my little purse to let myself out the door of my dorm. I had to hang up on her before I said something and hurt her feelings or admit the sole reason I decided to move out of state was to get away from the drama and the whole I need to go to church to make me a better person thing. I refuse to listen to her preach anymore about staying a virgin until I find the right church-going guy and get married.

My mother has this old-fashioned mentality that works great in some ways, but let's face it: we live in a modern era where men and women have casual sex. Love and marriage are not always part of the equation.

I walk toward the church to ease my guilt for hanging up on my mother but make a detour toward the cemetery. I haven't been by the grave since that first night, and I am kind of hoping someone left her flowers. I enter the gate and there is someone selling flowers that is about to pack up and leave for the day.

"Excuse me? Could you sell me one?"

I reach into my pocket for ten dollars and stick my hand out to the older woman.

She nods and holds out the bucket of different flowers, and I select the red roses for some reason—for love. I think when you die and someone takes the time to visit you, it is out of love and respect.

Even though I never knew the woman, it would be a nice gesture to place a bouquet of red roses on her grave. I remember the date of her birth on the marble headstone, and she died young.

After taking the money, she hands me the roses and leaves without a second glance. I head over to the grave with the flowers and notice that the single flower I had placed there the first time has already dried and wilted.

I look around and realize I'm the only one in the old cemetery. I kneel and brush the old flower away, wishing I had brought a bottle of water so I could have cleaned it. I scan the area, and my eyes land on an empty, clear container.

I look to see if there is a water spigot. I remember back home, in some of the cemeteries, they placed a water spigot so people could water the flowers or clean the headstones. Placing the flowers near the grave, I find the container, fill it with water, and return to clean the area the best I can. I see the little brass cup made for the flowers, fill it with water, and place the stems of the roses in without getting pinched by the thorns.

"Hi. It's me again. I hope you don't mind I cleaned up the place." I laugh to myself. "I brought you flowers. I hope that's ok."

I can't believe I'm talking to a dead person's grave that I don't even know.

I sit down, and for the next hour, I tell her what I couldn't tell my mother. I tell her about my parents and why I came here. I tell her about Jess and Dravin. I even told her how creeped out I was about what Valen said, but then I told her he was probably joking. It is like I trust this dead person even though they probably can't hear me and won't be able to talk back to me. Maybe that's why it feels so safe. There is no judgement. I couldn't go to confession about this stuff. The priest is a living person, and I just don't feel comfortable telling him my innermost sinful thoughts about a guy I'm crazy about but should stay away from. Far away.

"I don't know how to act around him. After Jess and I left his house, he didn't call. Then we saw each other in class and didn't call after that and I am too much of a coward to text him. I don't know if I should or even if I could. I figure his silence means that whatever we shared was just that, a one-time thing. He asked me if I could stay, and I did and that was the end of it."

I take a deep breath. I notice the sun is setting, and purple hues are beginning to fade in the sky. After sitting for almost two hours, I get up and stretch my limbs. The wind picks up, and I shiver, closing my jacket to keep me warm.

I make my way out of the cemetery and walk toward the church I haven't been to since I arrived.

I pull on the old handle, and the wooden door creaks when it opens. I smell flowers and candles. I look to my left and see three candles lit. I decide to light one for Jess, my mother, my father, the lady in the cemetery, and Dravin.

The bell inside the church chimes, signaling that it's already six in the evening. I look at the beautiful wood carvings. I look to my left and see the priest, and he nods. He isn't old, but he's not too young either, maybe in his early forties.

"Hello, welcome," he says.

"Hello. Do you have time for—"

He interrupts me. "For you, of course." He knows I want

to confess, but I find his answer odd. He nods and gets inside the wooden box.

I tell him about my call with my mother without going into detail, but he asks if I truly regret what I said and what I consider a sin under the eyes of God.

I can't answer and stay quiet. I change the subject and shift to my mother and how I lied about coming here. He tells me to ask God for forgiveness and to accept him. It is the most unusual confession I have ever had because this man doesn't seem like a priest. It is weird, and I know it is the last time I will come unless I decide to go to mass. I know different churches interpret things differently, and so do the priests, but this is weird.

A chill runs down my spine. It's like I feel my inner self warning me, telling me to leave and not to come here again. It's like this church isn't real but a mirage for something. Then, Marc's story about church and families. I get up to leave quickly and the priest notices that I'm nervous.

"Are you leaving so soon?" His eyes are black and blank, like he doesn't have a moral bone in his body. I suddenly feel like I told him things I shouldn't have.

"It's getting late."

"He's waiting for you," he says.

"What?"

"God."

I release the breath I was holding. He adjusts his collar like it burns him. I don't like him for some reason. Something is off about this church... about this whole place.

"Oh, right. Well. I'll pray in my room."

"You can pray right now. Right here." He points to where the statue of Jesus is crucified on the cross with its ancient wood carvings and beautiful intricate detail under the lights and stained-glass windows. The church is old and gorgeous. It is one of the most beautiful churches I have been inside of. I wish the people inside it matched the details of the church.

I wrap my jacket tighter around my body like a suit of armor. "I really must get going."

"If you must. If you need me, you know where to find me," he says.

And that right there is my cue to leave. "I gotta go."

His smile doesn't reach his eyes and it's like the devil himself is inside this church. I need to get the hell out of here. I'm already thinking about hell even while I'm inside a church that should make you feel safe and holy.

I practically run out the wooden door. The wind is whipping my hair and all I can hear is the sound of the trees swaying and groaning. The sky is almost black, and I hurry toward my dorm building. An eerie feeling keeps telling me to run. Something is not right about this place, or maybe I'm just paranoid. I check my phone and still haven't heard from Dravin since class. I have a missed text from Jess, though.

> Jess: Are you coming to the dorm? I've been waiting. Is everything ok?

I'm usually in my dorm room around this time. I haven't had dinner because I lost track of time at the cemetery, and then my guilt over the way I hung up on my mother led me to the church.

> Gia: I'll be right there.

> Jess: Ok.

CHAPTER TWENTY THREE

DRAVIN

I WALK into the church and notice almost an entire row of candles are lit. I'm walking further when I hear voices and giggling coming from the offices in the back.

I find the door closed and don't bother knocking. When it opens, I see a girl dressed as a nun, but what she is doing is nothing that an ordinary nun would be doing to a priest. Sucking and gurgling sounds can be heard as he bobs her head up and down in his lap. Getting a blow job dressed as a priest by a woman dressed as a nun, inside a church. That takes balls. I have seen fucked up shit in my day, but this is down-right…sinful.

Father Jacobs, as he prefers to be called, hasn't noticed me standing there because he is concentrating on his flaccid dick being sucked by a woman that doesn't understand the concept.

"Watch your teeth," he says. "I'm not going to say it again," he tells her in a hard tone.

"I'm sorry," she says.

"Get up," I tell her, my tone hard as ice.

"I need to talk to you, Jacobs. Hurry up and get out of here. Now," I demand.

The girl's eyes widen. "Dravin," she says with a worried look. She gets up and wipes her mouth, and I almost throw up in mine. I look away while both of them get it together. When I see they are clothed, I turn my head and face them again.

"Get out. My father and the others will be here shortly. Where is the real priest?"

"He isn't here. You know he is old and can't be here as long or stay late," Jacobs responds.

"Fine, whatever. I need to talk to you," I tell him.

"Is it about the girl?"

"You know it is," I growl.

When the fake nun, known as Tiffany, leaves, I make sure the door is closed and I stand in front of it while Jacobs swallows and looks around like someone is going to pop out and rescue him.

"She came to confession, and she told me about her mom. She also told me about a guy she met in school."

"What about him?

He adjusts his collar. "The normal attraction kind, but was more worried about how she hung up on her mom and the lie about coming to church."

"And?"

"Her mother. She must have a strenuous relationship with her mother and felt guilty for how she treated her today on the phone. Her parents are divorced."

"Did she give you a name when she told you about the guy?"

He shakes his head. "No. But it seemed she felt unsure and guilty about whatever happened between them. I asked her if she was ready to ask for forgiveness and she couldn't respond."

My nostrils flare. "Is that all?"

"Y-yes. Did I do something wrong?"

"Not yet, but I don't appreciate the way she left here running like she saw the devil inside the church. What else did you tell her?"

His eyes widen, and I know he was probably being a

creepy bastard, but one thing is for sure: He did me a favor by making her not want to set foot inside this church.

"T-that God is waiting for her."

I step forward. "He is. It's just not the God she thinks."

He steps back and his brow begins to sweat. Jacobs is a grimy bastard, but he is here to make sure no one walks into the church when the order is here having their secret meetings.

There are voices coming from outside the door.

"I think they are already here, Dravin."

I dismiss him and walk out to face the members of the order.

———

I walk out, and all the members take their seats in the pews. My father, along with Valen and Reid's fathers, take the places in the front like they are preaching the word of God. The most ruthless men are in this room. These meetings date back generations and are conducted in secret. They talk about a different order. Sins committed and how they should be punished under their rules. The rules being simple. If you go against their business dealings, you're out. An eye for an eye, if needed. They are all a bunch of ruthless liars who take wives for alliance purposes.

For centuries, these meetings were held by the three founding families. Reid's father, Valen's father, and my father, James Bedford. Warren is seated to the right and gives me a smirk that I return with a scowl. Fucking prick.

My father is the first to speak. "It has come to my attention that my son." He looks at me standing in the middle because I'm a smug bastard who refuses to sit. No one says anything because they don't want to be in one of the graves near the 1900s section of the cemetery. I'm not a good man. I'm the monster my mother tried to warn me about becoming. It's too late for me, but it's not too late for my Raven. She is all that matters right now.

"Dravin has lashed out at one of our own because of a girl. One of the Prey."

The Prey are the ones we've accepted that are not part of the order. The ones that don't have a father who is a member. We hunt them, play with them, and decide to let them pass when we see fit. The ones that make it, make the Forbes list and find good paying jobs. If they don't follow our rules and keep our secrets, they get eliminated. They die.

All the member's children attend Kenyan to ensure they follow the order. They learn to curb their appetites enough to not get caught. We fuck, we play, we kill if needed, but we are a secret alliance. Politicians, presidents, mayors, and governors are all in our pockets.

Centuries of wealth are passed down among the generations to unify us and make the order the strongest organization in the world. Money, power, and alliance are the mission of the order. You are either part of it through blood, married into it, or pledged by a higher member—meaning one of the three founders. Our women are chosen to breed, not for love. They have to come from wealthy families, of course, and be part of the order.

Faithfulness is not required, and love is not part of the union. But loyalty must be given, or they die. There are no women who make decisions in the order, only men. The women are protected by the man they choose to marry. If he allows it, then it can be done. If they go against the rules, they die. It is all straightforward.

The ones we consider the Prey eventually come to the church, and they confess. They try to pray to God for their transgressions and sins.

"My son felt he had to defend a girl's honor." He means I broke one of the member's son's hands, who is on the swim team, and it raises questions about my so-called instability since my mother's death. Or, as I like to put it, suicide.

"She is Prey."

My father's dark obsidian eyes, just like my right one, look to Warren.

"What do you have to say, Warren?"

"It is nothing but a misunderstanding. He obviously wants her and can't take the fact that she was interested in me first. It is nothing."

My father gives me an evil smirk. "We don't fight over Prey. We share if needed."

"He was with Veronica. I'm sure he needs time to rethink his decision."

Warren's face turns red, as if he is about to explode at the mention of Veronica. I was hoping they would make him marry the headcase, spiteful bitch.

My father smirks, and uneasiness slides down my spine. "I heard about the deal you made with her. She is loyal to the order, and if asked, she'd tell us what we need to know. I didn't think you would be interested in Veronica yourself. You do need to take a wife before you graduate."

My lip curls sardonically. "I don't want her." Warren smiles and I want to kill him, and I think I just might. Fuck what anyone thinks. I will soon take my spot at the top anyway. "Not interested."

Veronica's father is seated three rows down and huffs and

glares at me and Warren. No one wants to marry his crazy, sex-crazed daughter. I'm sure she has fucked half the school.

"Well, you must marry. All of you. Before your senior year is over."

The sons of the members are all seated. Reid is glaring at Garret. Valen is sitting like he could care less because he is the youngest of all of us. He has time to play. He just likes to play too much, and I'll be the first to teach him manners. Garret is not so bad but just got caught up with Veronica and her games.

The others must follow the order and whatever the three of us say, both on campus and off.

"I don't want you guys attacking each other unless it is voted on here."

Fat chance. Those rules don't apply to the sons of three families.

"What about this girl?"

My head snaps up and I roll my shoulders back. "What about her?"

"Is she a problem?"

"She's mine."

The room shifts and Warren's head snaps. "He hasn't had her, no one has."

"Not true."

My father raises his eyebrows at my declaration. I have never staked a claim on a Prey before. Everyone turns to face me, some members with their mouths parted.

"How so?"

"I fucked her."

Warren's nostrils flare and Valen coughs.

His eyes meet mine and I give him a stern glare. If he says otherwise, he knows I will rip him apart. If you stake your claim on a Prey, she's yours, and no one can touch her unless she wants it or you allow it.

This is the only way I can save her. The guys at school want her. I can smell it dripping in the church. The guys here are salivating. They feed off something or someone they cannot have. When men have a lot of money and are born rich, they get bored. Throw in a bunch of college kids with hard-ons into the mix, and you've got yourself a serious problem—especially ones who can get away with anything and are raised under the rules of the order.

No one will question me because they have yet to find a woman that would deny me. On the contrary, I have a problem trying to keep them from wanting more.

"Alright, since you've no doubt already tasted her. I guess the fun is over, or it has just begun."

My eyes find Warren, and his look is crystal clear. He wants Gia bad enough that he will overlook the fact that I've supposedly had her. Veronica was right about Warren. He has a hard-on for Gianna.

The topic ends regarding Gia and moves to other business issues: takeovers and mergers, who the major players are, and who is a liability to the order. It goes on for the next hour, and when the gauntlet is thrown, it is time to make my way out.

CHAPTER TWENTY FOUR

GIA

"YOU WERE AT THE CEMETERY?" Jess asks.

"Yeah, and then I went inside the church. Have you been?" I ask.

I wonder if she has met the creepy priest.

"I went once but have never gone again." She lowers her eyes and glances away. "I stopped going right before starting college."

Something must have happened to her for her to stop going or, worse, stop believing.

My phone buzzes on my nightstand, and I see it's a message from Dravin.

I'm surprised he texted me when I swipe up to read the message.

> Dravin: Are you in your room?

> Gia: Yes. Why?

> Dravin: Open the door.

I look up, and there is a knock on the door.

"Who could that be?" Jess asks.

I get up from the bed and smooth my long, dark hair. I'm still dressed in black leggings, thick socks, and a sweater. The only thing I took off was my cold-weather jacket.

I hold up my phone. "It's Dravin."

She quirks a brow and gives me a wide grin. "Look at you getting cozy with the bad boy of Kenyan."

I wave her off and open the door. Standing just outside in the hallway is a sinfully dressed Dravin. His eyes hold me hostage while I scroll over his fitted sweater under his jacket, which makes his double-wide shoulders look massive. He is so tall, and his angular jaw is defined. His eyelashes are so dark that you have to look closely to make sure he isn't wearing mascara. My eyes trail over his dark pants, which are a cross between jeans and slacks.

He rakes his fingers through his straight, dark hair. "Hi."

"Hi," I respond.

He licks his lips. "Do you want to go get something to eat?"

I smile and my heart begins to beat rapidly in my chest. "Are you asking me out on a date?"

"No."

My stomach sinks at how quickly he responds. Like I'm not good enough to go on a date with.

"Oh."

"I would have to be dating you to ask you that and everyone knows I don't date. I'm asking you if you want to get something to eat."

I flinch at how easily he can forget everything we've shared. How he thinks he can show up and I'm supposed to be honored that he is asking me to go anywhere with him. "I'm not that hungry, and I have a lot of homework," I say, trying to salvage my pride when it comes to him.

He furrows his brow and I raise mine just like Jess did a moment ago. "Is that all? Because I have to get back to studying."

He looks around me and he knows I wasn't studying. I

don't have my books out, and my bed is made. His eyes land back on mine. "I'm sorry. I know that came out wrong. I just—I'm not good at this sort of thing, alright? Please come with me? I want to eat with you."

I rub my lips together and contemplate whether I should or shouldn't go. Dravin blows hot and cold, though I shouldn't be so rude.

He didn't promise me anything, I remind myself.

"Alright. Let me put my boots on. Give me a minute."

His lips curl into a small smile. "Ok," he says. He leans in the room and turns to see a wide-eyed Jess. "Reid will stop by in fifteen," he tells her. "To make sure you're not alone."

I pinch my brows and glance at Jess, who just nods silently. I give her a smile and she starts to run her fingers through her curls. I inwardly grin because she is worried about how she will look when Reid shows up. I hope he likes her in a real sense and isn't taking advantage of her vulnerability. I like Jess, even though I think she comes from a fucked-up place. She really hasn't gone into detail, but you can tell something awful haunts her. She is just trying to purge it from her system. I can only hope a guy like Reid is the answer to her trouble and he doesn't hurt her more than she has been hurt by people in her past.

———

"I'm sorry about how I acted back there," Dravin says once we are in the back of the sedan that I notice is a Rolls Royce. I'm not familiar with cars driven by the wealthy, but there is just nothing like it. Once you have been in something this nice, you feel you have to know what it is. It also tells me that Dravin is beyond the normal lines of being a rich college kid

from a rich family. This is considered wealth. Old wealth.
The driven around kind of wealth you see in movies or
on TV.

"I get it. I know you aren't used to being this nice around
a girl."

"How would you know?" he teases.

"Someone texted me."

He laughs, and it's still the most contagious sound I have
ever heard. I never knew that a man's laugh could be considered beautiful. Everything about Dravin is beautiful, even his
darkness.

He chuckles low in his throat, a deep vibration that calls to
me. "You've got jokes," he says.

"I'm terrible at jokes, how about you?"

He gives me a side glance, "I'm more of a direct kind of
guy."

"I figured you would say that."

"Why is that?"

"I don't know. The way people fear you. They don't question anything you say or do."

"Is that so?"

"Oh, yeah. I've noticed."

He slides down on the seat, stretching his long, muscular
legs. "What else have you noticed?"

My breathing picks up, and I'm suddenly aware of him
and the way his voice gets deeper. "The way you look at me."

He shifts in the seat and presses a button to the privacy
screen and my heart skips a beat while it slides upward sepa-
rating us from the driver. His fingers slide into my hair behind
my ear. "How do I look at you, Raven?"

"L-like you've been waiting for me," I stammer.

He angles his head on the headrest like he is looking at the sky. Then he closes his eyes like he is thinking carefully about what he is going to say next.

At that exact moment, the car stops moving, and I can hear the driver's side door open. He straightens his head. "We're here," he says instead.

I peer out the window at a small restaurant just outside of town. The driver opens the door and Dravin gets out first and holds out his hand. I slide my fingers in his warm palm like a blanket protecting me from the cold chill outside.

The small restaurant looks like a bar with pool tables. It is a local fanfare, not at capacity but not empty either.

We are shown to a booth, and instead of him sitting across from me, he sits right next to me like we are a couple. The waitress comes to take our order, and her eyes widen when she sees Dravin. Her eyes find mine and she stares at the way Dravin's arm is stretched out behind me on the booth. If I moved an inch closer to him, I could feel the heat of his hard body. My stomach flutters and it is not from hunger. This happens to me every time I'm near him. I can't stop it. I can't control it.

The waitress is older and must know who Dravin is because she looks at him like someone she's seen before. "Hello, Mr. Bedford. Is this your girlfriend?"

"She belongs to me, and that's all you need to know."

"Of course, she does," she sasses, then turns to me. "What can I getcha, honey?"

"A grilled cheese and coke, please."

"One grilled cheese and coke coming right up."

She juts her hip out. "And you?" she asks Dravin, tapping her pen on the pad in her hand. The waitress is clearly annoyed with him, yet he doesn't correct or warn her like I have seen him do the others. He's just quiet. It seems she doesn't like his answer regarding me.

"I'll have what she's having," he finally says.

She glances at me and then at his arm draped over the back of the booth. "This is new," she says, walking away.

"I guess you come here often."

I'm not trying to sound like a jealous high schooler, but it is plain as day that he has brought other girls here with him. However, based on our waitress's reaction, I don't think that he usually sits this close or drapes his arms behind the booth.

"I'll be honest, I have."

I appreciate his honesty, but the butterflies quickly die a slow death in my stomach, replaced by shame for allowing myself to feel anything for Dravin. He is way out of my league, and I've come to realize this is the side of him that I have a problem with—a side of him that won't work for my poor heart.

"I understand."

I do understand now that I mean nothing to him. I'm a poor girl from Wisconsin, running from her divorced parents, trying to make something of myself in the real world. And all I ended up doing was falling for a guy who sees me as nothing but another girl he can say he fooled around with in college.

After ten minutes of silence, the food comes, but my appetite is gone. He begins to eat, but I push the food around my plate like a little kid, so it looks like I ate enough.

I think he feels the tension and stops eating, placing his cup of soda on the table.

He lowers his head and takes a deep breath. "I don't know what to say when people ask if you're my girlfriend. I have never had one before. I-I don't want to hurt you. I'm sorry."

He turns in the booth to face me and cups the side of my

cheek with his clean hand. His lips are inching closer, and I close my eyes.

He brushes his lips gently over mine and says, "All I know is that you belong to me. It is what I feel and what I know."

I whimper softly when his tongue darts and licks the seam of my lips. My lips part, and I can feel his breath on my lips. My eyes remain shut for fear if I open them, the moment will be ruined, and he will stop.

I hear a throat clear and my eyes open to find the waitress standing near our table. "I can see that you do belong to him. This is a first."

She leans close to the table, acting like he is not right there listening to what she is going to say. "I always knew there would be one to make him do crazy shit he normally wouldn't." She gives me a wink. "So, you're the one."

Dravin smirks. "Stop scaring her, Dorothy."

"Oh, I'm not. Your momma would have loved to see this, God rest her soul. She's gorgeous, Dravin. You did good this time. Not like those other hussies you parade around with. I like this one."

"I like this one, too," he says, taking a sip from the straw.

"From the looks of it, I bet you do."

"Give him hell, sweetheart. Make him work for it."

Dravin chuckles. "Oh, she does. Trust me, she's worth it."

My heart sings at his praise and I feel warm all over again. He nods his head to my plate. "Eat."

I take a bite of the sandwich and smile at Dorothy."

"That a girl. I like that you order real food. You're not some rabbit eating skinny twig a second away from becoming anemic."

I like Dorothy. She reminds me of a wise grandmother.

She doesn't look too old but she can easily be borderline grandmother material. If she isn't, she will be one day.

When she walks away, I ask, "She knew your mother?"

I feel him stiffen slightly at the mention of his mother, but he nods. "Yeah, my mother and I would come here twice a week when my father had business to attend to."

"You were close?"

"Very close. I was closer to my mother than my father. He hated it in some way because he wanted me to follow in his footsteps. He knew I was going to anyway. He required it of me. He just didn't like my mother's depression. She suffered from it for a long time."

I nod. "If you don't mind me asking, how did she die?"

"She committed suicide. I found her in the tub in a pool of blood."

My stomach drops and the mood dimmed at the mention of something so tragic. It is like the life has been sucked out of the restaurant.

"I'm sorry. I can't imagine what that was like."

Then a thought occurs to me and before I stop myself, I blurt, "Is your mother buried in the cemetery?"

He wipes his mouth with the napkin and places it over his plate. "Yes."

Oh my God. I have been talking to his mother about everything. About him. I think I knew deep down that she was his mother or related. Her last name is the same, but she is buried alone in an old cemetery, and he doesn't bring her flowers.

No one brings her flowers.

"Why didn't you tell me that night in the cemetery?"

"Because I didn't want you to know why I was there."

"I accused you of stalking me."

"And I corrected you, but you didn't want to believe me."

"I'm sorry.

"Don't be. And thank you."

I lick my lips and fidget with the napkin in my hand. I lower my head. "For what exactly?"

"For sitting with her and for buying her flowers. No one has ever done that for her besides me."

My eyes find his and all I see is pain. A deep pain that tears at your soul. Not just because he lost his mother so tragically but because no one visits her grave. His father never loved his mother. He doesn't go there to visit her. Her own husband doesn't bring her flowers. My heart bleeds for his mother. I can only imagine loving your son, knowing that your husband and his father never loved you. It would take a very strong woman to have dealt with that pain.

"She must have been a very strong woman. And she must have loved you very much."

He nods and my heart continues to break. It all makes sense. The way he is withdrawn. The reason he chooses to live alone. The pain I see in the depths of his eyes and the fact that he was taught not to believe in love. What I don't understand is, what kind of monster teaches his son not to believe in love. But I know the answer. The type of monster to have driven his wife to a depression so deep she felt she had no choice but to commit suicide.

He motions for Dorothy and settles the bill. She gives me a wink and I grin in response. The silence stretches between us like a rubber band about to snap. I don't know what to say or do next because his neck muscles are tense, and he has this tic in his jaw like he is at war with something.

"Let's go. I have to get you back," he says.

On the way back inside the luxurious car, there is a center

console wedged between us, and I make the decision to comfort him. The cabin is quiet, and I look at the privacy screen, but it remains closed. He scrolls through his phone, and "Ghost" by Badflower plays on the speakers. I take my jacket off and I straddle his lap. He slides his hands under my sweater slowly up my shirt and I take his lips between mine and suck the top then the bottom. I slide my hands over his chest, my fingers tracing the dips of his stiff muscles.

I feel the hardness of his erection between my legs, and I gasp at how hard he is for me. His cock is like a hot metal searing me through his pants. He lowers his head and pulls my bra hard enough so that my nipple escapes the cup. He takes it into his mouth, sucking, causing electricity to snake all over my body. My clit throbs seeking a release only he knows how to give me. I grind my hips rubbing myself over his cock in a rhythm that has a hiss escaping his breath as it fans my swollen nipple.

He grips my hips, and my fingers slide in his thick dark hair, his face eye level with my chest. He looks up, and I can feel his pain radiating from him, and I'll do anything to soak it up and take it away. I grab his wrist, the one with the scar that he made trying to end his life like his mom. I kiss along the scars, small kisses, sliding my tongue up and down the wound like it is leaking blood. Tattoos hide the evidence of his agony, but not from me. The deep scar from a cut inflicted out of pain. Proof that even monsters hurt in the darkness of their hell.

The car stops, and I know the driver will open the door any second. My head angles closer to give him a kiss. As soon as the driver opens the door, I rip my lips from his, grab my jacket, and slide off his thighs, leaving him inside the car with his chest rising and falling. I run as quickly as I can with the cold whipping me in the face. The burn of the frigid air cooling my burning cheeks until I'm safely inside my dorm. My eyes scan Jess's bed, and for once, I'm glad that it is empty and I'm alone.

I look down as my phone buzzes.

> Dravin: Are you safely inside your room?"

> Gia: Yes.

I stare at my phone screen, hoping he will text me. Hoping he will tell me to come back outside or that he is at my door. After ten minutes, I give up and lay on my bed staring at the ceiling, my lips curling into a smile because I know deep down that I mean more to Dravin than any other girl he has ever been with.

CHAPTER TWENTY FIVE

DRAVIN

GIA IS FAR from being plain, but she isn't the type that would lift her skirt in the bathroom of a bar and get fucked against the bathroom stall by yours truly. I'm usually a good judge of character, but with her, I've got it all wrong. Every time I'm with her, I want to bend her over and fuck her hard, but then, something stops me. It feels wrong to treat her that way. I shouldn't care, but I do.

She's like fresh blood in a pool full of vampires. She screams innocence. Her soft skin and the smell of her arousal make my blood boil in a heat that goes straight to my cock. If I slide into her, I know I will take her hard. I'll take her hard the first time, then the second, and the third. When I'm almost done, on the fourth round, I'll go slow and gentle until she feels she can't take it anymore, until she's begging me for mercy. Begging me to never stop.

I look over at my mother's grave, cleaned by my Raven, with a bouquet of red roses. The roses of love. It is like she knew since the first time I saw her put a rose on my mother's grave that my mother died due to the love that was missing from the man who was supposed to love her and protect her. It is like she knew my mother loved red roses. All my father did was show my mother how much he didn't love her, and it killed her. My father thinks her suicide was because she was weak. He told me that is a prime example of how love makes you weak. Because it destroys you. But really, he destroyed her, not love. It was not having love that killed my mother.

It happened during my senior year of high school, right after I turned eighteen. My father knew she did it deliberately when I became a legal adult because everything that was hers, she left to me as her sole beneficiary. They overlooked the blood, and her wrist slit vertically. They overlooked the fact that she tried to commit suicide. She knew what she was doing but actually died from drowning in the tub. My father had it covered up and had reported to everyone that she slipped, hit her head, and drowned.

Why had she done it? A broken heart. The lack of love from my father. She didn't leave a letter. All she left me was money and lots of it. My mother came from a wealthy, predominant family, as required to be married to a founding member of the order.

There isn't much family on either side. My parents were only children, but they made sure to carry out the tradition.

My father places a lot of demands and pressure on me, but the truth is, since my mother left me close to a billion dollars, I've rebelled. I don't need him or the order.

CHAPTER TWENTY SIX

GIA

I CHECK my phone for the eighth time hoping to see a text from Dravin. After the ninth time, I check the time and it is after eleven in the morning. It is cold outside. I shower and get dressed. I notice that Jess never made it home last night but she sent the only text I woke up to this morning telling me that she was ok. I guess she had fun last night.

Determined to talk to Dravin, I order an Uber to go to his house. I know I'm acting like a crazy chick starving for attention, but I want answers. I want to know if we are friends or if we are more. I want to know why he blows hot and cold. One minute, he wants me, and the second he gets a dose of me, he ghosts me until he needs another small dose of me, and it starts all over again. The mixed signals. The way he opened up about the death of his mother is a subject I know he doesn't talk to anyone about. So why me? Why does he trust me with his pain? Why hasn't he tried to seduce me like he did before and ask me for sex? It is like he is holding back all of a sudden.

He let me go in the shower and in the car last night. He didn't go after me. I feel like I'm going out of my mind. I shouldn't want him, but I do. I want to feel him completely inside me. I want my body to melt with his. I want to show him that there is love where there is pain. I want him to be my first.

My index finger tingles when I press the button of the doorbell to his imposing house. I hear the sound of footsteps coming toward the front door. The door opens, and a shirtless Dravin is at the door in all his glory. Tattoos over hard muscles rippling with every breath he takes. His biceps flex as he bends his arm to hold the door open.

"I need to talk to you," I say quickly.

He moves so I can come inside. I barge my way through his house to the living room, noticing the fireplace is lit, and it is suddenly too warm. I take off my jacket, gloves, and scarf. I remove my sweater, and I'm left in just my tank top.

His eyes smolder when he notices I'm not wearing a bra. My chest rises and falls from the effort of removing my clothes too fast and the worry about what I'm going to say.

"Why didn't you come up? Why didn't you call this morning? Why do you blow hot and cold with me?"

He quirks a brow. "Is that why you came here? To question me? I thought you weren't the type to get fucked in a bathroom or against the pillar in a cemetery? He steps closer. "Because we both know that is what would have happened if you would have said yes."

My nostrils flare in annoyance. "How about the pool or the shower or the car? We both know you don't bring girls in your room or in your shower."

He leans close, his lips inches from mine. "Are you trying to tell me you wanted me to fuck you in my shower and in my pool?"

"You asked if it was ok and I said I wanted you. So, what are we? Friends, lovers—" I trail off.

His eyes are doing that thing again, battling. He tilts his head, and his eyes darken. I should just leave; this was a mistake. Like when you prep yourself for a confrontation, only when you are actually there do you realize you were overthinking things.

"I don't believe in love and we both know I'm not friends with girls. Last night was all you."

My heart clenches in my chest, and a sinking feeling from his rejection pulls me down. He doesn't want me. He is right; this is all me and my fantasy. I want someone who is emotionally unavailable. "I gotta go."

I turn to leave before I break down in front of him, before he sees how I feel about him and how much I have fallen for him.

"Gia," he growls.

I stop, my body tensing. I close my eyes, the want for him running through my veins. The need to finally have him. I turn around and run into his arms. He catches me. My legs wrap around his waist as his lips crash with mine. Our tongues battling, pulling, coming apart, again and again. My arms wrap around his neck like a vine. He walks to the front of the fireplace on the plush carpet and lays me down, peeling every piece of clothing off my body until I'm naked, with him between my legs. He looks down at me, and I'm lost in his ocean depths, as if I were walking from the shore to the unknown.

His tongue licks the valley between my breasts up to the base of my throat, up over my chin to my mouth. His mouth brushes over mine and his tongue licks my bottom lip then my tongue. My hips lift, seeking his warmth. He kisses my jaw and neck, and I slide my hands up his back, feeling the muscles ripple beneath my fingers.

I shiver and look down between my legs and then I tense. He glances up and licks his lips. His brows are pinched, and it dawns on him that I'm inexperienced.

"Is this your first time?" he asks hoarsely.

My eyes find his and I bite my lip. "Yes."

He raises himself with one hand and looks down between my legs and then slowly back up. "Are you sure you want it to be me?"

I nod and he gets up and removes his sweats. He walks over and comes back, tearing the wrapper of the condom with his teeth, and places it over his hard cock with his piercing and angry veins. His face is close to my neck, and he turns his head and whispers in my ear. "You tell me if you want me to stop, ok?"

"Okay," I say softly, almost above a whisper.

My head tilts up and I close my eyes when he sees that I'm ready by placing two fingers inside me. He stretches me and I clench. He keeps repeating the motion over and over again until I'm dripping. I can feel the drops of my arousal as it drips to the back of my ass. He slides in one finger, finger fucking me, and the noise mixes with the crackling of the fire. Like the burning flames right next to me, I'm burning to feel him inside of me. He settles between my legs, and the head of his cock enters me, slowly breaching my tight folds. The air charges all around us as he slides in inch by inch. He pulls out slowly and I can tell he is holding back from the way he tenses. His elbows are on each side of my head, and he is holding both of my hands.

"Don't look away from me," he whispers.

He pushes in again, and I gasp when he breaks my barrier. He stills inside me, and I try to not close my eyes at the pain. "I'm sorry," he says tenderly, kissing my forehead, but the pain gradually goes away and is replaced by need. My clit pulses and he can feel it because he moves inside me, picking up the pace.

I moan his name. "Dravin."

I arch my back and he sucks one nipple and then the other.

My body begins to glisten with sweat. His sweat drips in between us and mixes with my arousal.

"More," I plead.

My legs open wider and he responds by grinding into me. "You're so beautiful," he says. "Perfect."

I grind my hips seeking more and he fucks me. He begins to fuck me so good. I feel the piercings on his cock, rubbing, and I gasp.

"More, Dravin. Please."

He grips my thighs and begins to pound into me. My breasts bounce with each forceful thrust.

"Oh, God. Yes," I say on a moan.

His lips lift with a smile. My climax builds and builds until he thrusts one last time. "I'm coming, Dravin. Oh, God. I'm coming. My pussy grips his cock and I can feel him grunt and lose himself.

"Gia," he groans while his cock spasms spilling inside the condom. He stills for a minute and stares into my eyes.

My lips part, and when I lift my head to seek his lips, he pulls away, his eyes darkening like a curtain masking the windows of his soul. He pulls out and gets up, leaving me on the rug. I cover my naked breasts and turn to see him walk into the kitchen. I sit up, embarrassed he left me there. When I think he's going to come back, he doesn't. He stops at the stairs, and my heart hollows out. Tears begin spilling down my cheeks.

He wouldn't. I shake my head. Not like this. My lower lip trembles. He doesn't even glance at me. He faces the staircase while my heart breaks into a million pieces. Then, he begins to head toward his room.

"There's a bathroom next to the front door. "You can see yourself out."

My heart drops. The tears begin to flow like the blood leaking from between my thighs. I gaze down at the mess and my eyes widen in horror at the stain on the rug. Not caring, I get up on shaky legs and look around to find my clothes. I sniff, my eyes blinded by the tears that won't stop. I pull my underwear over my thighs like a band-aid covering a gaping wound, not wanting to be here a second longer. I grab my phone and look at it like a bomb waiting to detonate.

I wipe my cheeks and look up at the stairs, hoping this is a joke or that he will change his mind, but my shoulders jump when I hear his door close with a thud. I go to the kitchen and clean the rug the best I can, angry tears scarring my cheeks, but I give up because no matter how much I scrub, the rug is stained and ruined, just like me.

———

The water flows down my body, washing the memory of him away. The same way he slipped through my fingers. I knew deep down that this was my fate, but stubbornly, I wanted to see if I could fix his broken parts. I wanted to show him that it's possible for someone to love you even if you're damaged. But I was wrong. I gave myself to him willingly, and I know at heart this isn't the end of my suffering. Like a predator that has finally lured and captured his Prey, wounding them until all that is left is the pain that will soon take over. This is where my pain begins. Instead of being protected, I was hunted and now I must pay for being naïve.

For trusting the beautiful words on a card. The simple gift of a rose. Hoping that it came from a place deep in his soul. I let myself be lured into the lies. It is funny how there are no flaws when there's hope. There wasn't a single flaw in his words, but I guess that is what makes a great liar—a great deceiver. And I played right into it. I missed all the signs. All I can do is learn from it. I learned what love feels like and it took him breaking me to understand it. Every touch, every kiss, every breath felt like a lettered kiss. His eyes warned me of the beautiful storm that was coming. Deep down, I knew, but I let my heart lead me where I shouldn't have gone. Now, all that is left are the broken pieces—the pieces I will pick up. I will toss the parts away that remind me of him because that is all I can do to save me from myself.

CHAPTER TWENTY SEVEN

DRAVIN

THE DOORBELL RINGS, and I check the camera to see who is at the door. I rake my fingers through my hair. I haven't slept in forty-eight hours. It has been two days since Raven left. Even if what happened was cruel, it would be worse to tell her the truth. The truth of who I am and how she was a bet to begin with. She doesn't need someone like me in her life. She deserves to graduate from here and find someone to share her life with. Someone that isn't fucked up. I tried to fight it, but I knew if she wanted me, I wouldn't deny her. I backed out like a pussy in the shower and then in the car. I have tried, but I couldn't deny her. She is like a priceless vase that I have destroyed.

I open the door and look at the box. I pick it up and check to see if it is addressed to anyone. Except there are no labels or names written anywhere. Once I place it on the counter, I open it and feel the knife rip through me—gutting me.

The clothes, the card, and even the phone I gifted my Raven are neatly placed in the box. I grip the phone and press the button to power it on, but it is completely erased. I drop it inside the box like it burned my hand. I fish out my phone and try to dial her number, but it's disconnected. I keep trying, but the same dial tone pops up. I tell myself it's for the best.

It is the best scenario, but I know deep down it's a lie.

My Raven is gone.

CHAPTER TWENTY EIGHT

GIA

I CHANGED my number and got a basic phone. Nothing like the one Dravin got me, but an older model. It was all I could afford, and I decided to venture on my own and get it under my name, ultimately changing my number. My mother and father were upset, but I told them eventually, I needed to get a new number and save them from having to split the bill. I immediately blocked Dravin's number. Everything happens for a reason, and I wanted to make sure that if Dravin got my number, he couldn't get through to me.

The best way to get over someone or something is to remove all memories of them from your life and try to replace them with better ones. Ones that put a smile on your face. I went to the cemetery after I got the phone and I cried on his mother's grave. I needed to cry to someone, and I knew that my own mother would never understand. She would think some occult possessed me or something, and I refuse to be the type of daughter who always shuns her mother and hangs up on her.

"Hey, are you ok?" Marc asks me in the library.

I plaster a fake smile. "Yeah, why?

His lips form a thin line. "You haven't seen it, have you."

I tilt my head from where I'm sitting at the check-out desk.

"Seen what?"

"Jess probably hasn't seen it, or I'm sure she would have shown you."

Getting annoyed. I swallow and roll my eyes. "Marc, what are you talking about?"

He pulls out his phone and hands it to me. I take it, and it opens to the school social page, where there is a chat open.

> Lizzy: Did you hear that Dravin won the bet that he could fuck the new girl. He obviously won. Veronica was appalled that the virgin ruined his rug. We all know Dravin Bedford never fucks a girl in his bed.

My eyes widen when I see a clear picture of the soiled rug I tried to clean up. It was ruined, and I wanted to get out of there as quickly as possible to shower in the dorm and away from Dravin. Heat radiates through my neck and cheeks as it hits home. I was a bet.

Tears well up in my eyes, but what did I expect? This is Dravin, and everyone warned me, including Marc. I was a fucking bet. It all makes sense. The bathroom, the cemetery, the pretty notes, the flowers. It wasn't just a lie, but a game, and I was the pawn.

I read the next line.

Melissa: There is only one girl he has never been able to sleep with that he desperately wants, and it's Veronica. Everyone knows that. They're perfect for each other. The perfect challenge. She is perfect in the eyes of everyone.

"I'm sorry, Gianna. I tried to warn you, but that's what he does. What they all do. You're not the first."

My teeth snag my bottom lip to keep it from trembling. The chat says the new girl, but that is how they keep from getting in trouble. There are no names, except everyone on campus knows I'm the new girl.

I hand the phone back, and now I know how Jess must

have felt, but this is ten times worse because I fell for him.

"Are you ok? Gianna. I'm so sorry."

I look up at Marc, and he must see how hurt I feel, but I keep a straight face and lie. "I'm fine. It's not like he was my boyfriend or anything."

My eyes blink and his mouth pulls into a frown. "Do you want me to get you anything?"

I shake my head. "I just want to be alone right now," I tell him in a shaky breath.

"I'm here for you, Gia. If you need anything or someone to talk to… I'm here."

"Thank you. I need to get going or I'm going to be late for poetry."

I walk into the class, and the professor is already there, and he gives me a curt nod. I ignore all the knowing glances cast my way. I even ignore the whispers and the snickers. I won't let it get to me. This is my fault, and I only have myself to blame. I raise my chin and sit in a seat in the far corner of the auditorium-style room. I noticed on the first day that it was always empty, giving me an aerial view of the entire class and preventing anyone from sitting behind me.

When the class is about to begin, Dravin walks in. It's funny when you are hurting and the person who hurt you is in the same room. All the hateful words you conjure in your head pause, and when you try to find the flaws in their appearance, you can't. It proves that you still have feelings for them. It proves—I still have feelings for Dravin.

He finds a seat and faces forward. I'm not sure if he knows I'm here or not, but it doesn't matter because his attention is on the girl who waved at him the first day. Marc walks in and his eyes scan the room until they land on mine. He gives me a grin and a wave.

I'm frozen in my seat because heads begin to turn my way, and I want to curse him for causing unwanted attention. I lower my head and wave at him like nothing is amiss, like my heart isn't breaking, as I watch Dravin look over at me and then at Marc like he could care less.

"Everyone is here," The professor announces. "I will call on a few of you to read a page from your journals." His eyes scan the room, and I lower my head, letting my hair slide forward like a black curtain. I hope and pray he doesn't call on me. "Gianna."

FML. I look up and ignore the eyes cast my way. I flip the pages of my journal until I reach the last entry.

"I look in the mirror.

All my pieces are shattered.

I look closer and I wonder if my soul is on the other side.

I look inside me and I'm empty, full of lies and betrayal.

All I do is bleed and bleed.

Am I that insignificant?

Am I the sacrifice?

The soft-spoken words written as the ink dries, whispering death on poisoned lips.

I'm alone as you are no more.

My wings will heal, and I will fly away—never to be seen again."

The room goes deathly silent. You could hear a pin drop. I look up and refuse to look over at Dravin. I will never look into his eyes ever again.

"Raven?" I hear his soft-spoken voice, but I don't look, and I don't answer. It is like he is a ghost. An imaginary shadow I made up in my mind and in my head. Even if he haunts me in my dreams, I refuse to acknowledge him when I'm awake.

"Look at me," Dravin demands quietly.

There is this thing about ghosts I read somewhere. You don't have to acknowledge them when you don't want to. In this case, Dravin Bedford has become my ghost. Like the Raven, here one minute and gone the next.

———

The next three weeks are all the same—school, dorm, and sleep. Repeat. I ignore the black roses on my bed every week and throw them out. I ignore the unknown text messages.

> Unknown: It's me. Dravin
>
> Unknown: Are you ok?
>
> Unknown: I'm sorry.
>
> Unknown: You looked pretty in class today.
>
> Unknown: Please answer me.

Every week is the same string of messages. I ignore all of them the same way he ignored me after I gave myself to him and he threw me away.

"Is it him again?" Jess says from across the room.

"Yeah," I answer, staring up at the ceiling. "I block the number and he figures out a way to call me from another one. It's the same thing every week."

"Did he say he was sorry?"

"Yeah, but I don't care. He got what he wanted and won the bet. I don't get what his problem is? I have left him alone."

"I think that's it, though." She turns on her side, and I do the same, so we are face to face across the room on our small beds. "No one has ever ignored Dravin before. He isn't used to it."

"He needs to get used to it because I don't want to see him ever again."

"I get it. You don't have to say anymore," she sighs. "Do you want to go get a couple of drinks at the Babylon? You've been cooped up in this room every day. You're going to turn into a moth pretty soon."

I give her a grin.

"Come on. Maybe you can talk to a cute guy and forget all about him."

I lay back down and close my eyes. "That's the thing. There isn't a guy who can compete with Dravin."

She giggles. "True, but you're going to have to make an exception sooner or later. Forget about him. What he did to you was next level of fucked up even for me. You gave him your virginity, and he exploited it like a trophy. He could have just told you he wasn't interested and moved on."

"I don't think he really liked being with me. He wouldn't look at me after. It was like I disgusted him." My eyes well up in tears. "I let him screw me on a rug like a dog. My first time wasn't even on a bed. He didn't even ask if I was ok after." I say hoarsely, my voice breaking.

"He doesn't deserve you, Gianna. I know a guy that looks like Dravin makes a girl want to try and mold him into this good guy, but the truth is, he just isn't capable, and nothing or no one will change him. Especially the sons of Kenyan. They take. They don't give. You can't lose yourself because you decided to take the risk."

I slam my hands to my side, turn my head, and face her once more. "Alright, I'll go. Let's get out of here."

She smiles, "Atta girl."

CHAPTER TWENTY NINE

GIA

WE SLIDE into the booth at Babylon. It's a Friday night, and the place is full of college students. I avoid looking at the billiard tables because that's where Dravin and the swim team love to hang out.

I'm facing away from the pool tables, and I glance at Jess, who is looking behind me. "Well, don't turn around because he is there, and he is pissed. He is having words with Veronica and her white skin is red like a tomato.

"I could care less. She can have him, and he can have her."

I know it's a lie, but sooner or later, I have to get over Dravin. I have to accept that I got played like a violin. The stares and smirks aimed my way have calmed down, but I still get the feeling I'm being watched—Preyed upon.

Two young guys in Ohio State hoodies stop by our table. One guy smiles at me, and the other at Jess. "Hey, ladies. Are you two here with anyone?"

I look at Jess and she winks at me with a smile. "We're just having a couple drinks after a long week."

The good-looking one, the one who looks like James Dean, holds out his hand. "I'm Kyle, and this is Dillon. We figured you ladies needed company. It's a shame you two are seated over here by yourselves while the rest of the guys from your school hang out with the groupies."

"How do you know we don't attend Ohio State?"

He slides in next to me and places the beer in his hand

next to my vodka and cranberry. Dillon slides in and takes a seat next to Jess and smiles.

"We know this because we would have noticed you two."

His eyes gleam with laughter and I smile. "Of course, you would say that."

A dark shadow looms and the hairs on my neck stand up. Kyle peers over and Dravin, Reid, and Valen are standing near the end of the table. "You're in my seat," Dravin says in an icy tone directed at Kyle.

Kyle looks at me. "I think you're mistaken." He turns his head and whispers in my ear. "What's your name?"

I give him a grin, avoiding looking at Dravin, and tell him, "Gia."

"Gia and her friend didn't walk in with you, and she would have told me if she had been with you when I asked." He points behind him to the pool tables. "You three were engrossed in your game of pool with your girls over there."

Dravin's lip snarls. "Get up, or I'll throw you out."

Kyle smirks. "Oh, yeah. I know who you are."

"The three sons of Kenyan. The order. We know all about you and your organization. Don't think for a second people don't know who you guys are. We also know that these girls aren't part of your little circle and are fair game," Dillion chimes in.

The order? What the fuck is the order. Jess glances at me and then at Reid. Reid's fists are clenched, and Valen is grinning like the Joker, ready for a fight.

"I suggest you run along before you disappear," Reid says in a hard tone, referring to Kyle and Dillion.

"Stop it," I snap. "Leave us alone. We have left you alone. You got what you wanted."

"No," Dravin quips.

He grabs Kyle by the neck and pulls him forcefully, and like a rag doll, he slides him off the booth and drops him onto the ground.

"What the fuck, Dravin? Stop it."

I get up and I'm in his face. His eyes are lethal and full of darkness. He is breathing hard. "No."

"Yes." I pause and lift my chin defiantly. "I don't want you." He flinches. "You got what you wanted from me. Now, fuck off. I have left you alone. I don't want anything from you. I'm not your friend; I'm not your girlfriend or your fuck buddy. I'm nothing to you," I seethe. I look over at Veronica and her cronies. I point to her. "He's all yours, Veronica. You can bet on that."

Dravin shakes his head. "No. Don't say that. You don't know what you're saying." His jaw is tight. "Raven, please."

I walk closer and ignore the need to crush him to me. I ignore the smell of his hypnotizing scent and the way his shirt is melted on his muscled frame. I ignore the shameless want pooling between my thighs. "I don't want you. I'd rather be someone's whore than be with you."

He clenches his teeth. "Don't say that."

"Why, because it's honest? At least I know what I'm in for. I won't be a bet or a joke. I will be their whore. Because with you, I was less than that."

He tries to lift his hand to touch my face, and I step back. The tears burning behind my eyes that I refuse to let fall. I look down where Kyle is rubbing the back of his neck.

"Are you ok?" I ask.

He didn't deserve for Dravin to toss him from the booth like that. He didn't do anything wrong except try to make me smile. I move to the side and Dravin's hand shoots out to grab me.

I snap my arm back. "Don't touch me. I've spent hours scrubbing you off my skin."

"Damn," Valen mutters.

Dravin's eye twitches. For a second, I see guilt, but then a functioning part of my brain tells me a guy like Dravin is incapable of the emotion.

"Let's go, Jess. It was a mistake coming here," I say, walking back.

Jess gets up and Reid follows her movements with a sneer. "We're taking you home."

"No," Jess says.

"Yes," Dravin says, moving forward.

Jess and I walk out of the bar, and I'm surprised no one stops them from following us.

When we make it outside, we see a black SUV parked out front, its driver waiting with the door open.

"Get in. It isn't safe."

"What are you talking about?"

"Get in! Jesus, woman. Get inside the car."

I get in with Jess, Valen, and Reid."

"They don't know, Dravin. She doesn't know."

"Know about what?" I ask, clearly annoyed. I rub my hands together from the cold.

Dravin slides his hands over mine and I tear them away. "Don't touch me, asshole."

"I will touch what belongs to me."

I laugh sarcastically. "Yeah, in your dreams. Set the water to cold. You're going to need the cold shower."

Valen chuckles, scratching his brow. "You really hit me in the face for what I said to her that day in the kitchen, when she hates you," Valen tells Dravin.

Dravin hit Valen? For what he said to me? How did he know what he said that day?"

"You deserved it. I thought you and Reid probably told him." I tell him.

"We didn't tell him shit. I figured you did." Valen says.

I throw my hands up. "I don't talk to him much. Plus, I don't think he cares. He shouldn't matter."

"It matters," Dravin chimes in, looking out the window.

I roll my eyes. "Could have fooled me."

The SUV stops, and I realize we are not in the dorm but at Dravin's house. My head whips to him. "Take me home."

He looks at me. "You are home."

He gets out. Reid ushers Jess inside without a word, Valen trailing behind him.

I climb out of the SUV, stomping into the house and out of the cold weather. I walk into the living room and remove my jacket because I'm hot and I don't like to sweat. I'm also pissed off.

"So where this time? The couch, maybe, or the dining room table?"

"Knock it off, Raven."

He takes his jacket off and removes his sweatshirt. His muscles ripple under his black tank top. I take a step back to keep me from wanting to run my fingers down his arms.

I look around and notice he replaced the rug. Then I lick my lips and get closer.

"Want me to ruin the new one?"

He looks over at where I'm pointing to the new rug. His eyes harden and he walks me back to the wall. "You want to push me. I'm sorry for what happened. It was Veronica who got in here and took the picture of the rug. I did tell everyone that I slept with you so they would back off. I was claiming you. Protecting you."

"Claiming me? What am I an object?"

"No, you're Prey."

He grabs my hand and pulls me up the stairs until we end up in his room.

I gasp. "What?"

He walks over and moves the mouse so that his screens turn on, takes a seat in his chair, and motions for me to move forward.

He moves his finger like a hook and pats his thigh. "Sit. I have to show you something."

"Why? I can stand right here. I'm not blind."

He runs his fingers through his dark hair and blows a puff of air out of his cheeks.

"Fine." He gets up.

I back up toward the door nervously. When I'm close enough to the door, I can hear Jess moaning. My eyes find his and they freeze. We can hear her moaning while Reid is fucking her. Valen is groaning while she must be sucking him off. My pussy gets wet, and I feel it dripping between my thighs. My nipples strain under my long-sleeved sweater.

"Get on the bed," he demands. "Take off your pants and open your legs."

"No."

He walks closer. "I can smell how much you want me, Raven. I want to taste you."

Holy fucking Christ. My pussy throbs just thinking about his tongue and what it would feel like. He gets closer, lifting my chin as he angles his head so his lips are a breath away from mine. "I want to taste that sweet pussy. Tell me you don't want to feel my tongue fuck your sweet cunt,

Raven. I can smell how wet you are for me." He licks my closed lips.

It is the most erotic and filthy thing I have ever heard or felt. "Why?" Why are you doing this to me?"

His eyes darken. "Because, I want more. I can't let you go, Raven." He slides his hand and cups my pussy over my leggings and flicks his finger over the seam where my pussy splits. "You feel this pussy." I nod my head slowly, my eyes half open. "It is mine. I will break you and then put you back together and break you again. It doesn't matter how many times I break you because when I put you back together, we will fit perfectly."

He slides his hand inside the band of my leggings and swipes his finger between my slit. A whimper escapes from my lips and he licks my lips after the sound escapes. "I taste it, Raven. I can taste the need." His finger runs the nub of my clit and it throbs. "I can feel it."

He slides his finger through my pussy. I'm hot and drenched between my legs.

"So wet. So pretty," he whispers.

My heart is beating...hard. I stop hearing Jess moan and can only hear the sound of his breath and the beating of my heart.

He removes his hand and slides my pants off along with my boots. He lifts the hem of my sweater, removing it in one swoop. My clothes pool on the floor. I'm left in my lace bra. He slides the straps down until the tops of my nipples peak but doesn't remove it.

He licks one nipple and then the other. "Dravin," I gasp.

He chuckles. "Get on my bed and open your legs so I can see that pussy and how much it wants me to suck it dry."

I sit on the bed and open my legs. My cheeks heat at how

vulnerable I feel. He removes his tank top, and his muscles flex and move, causing me to clench my thighs.

"You want me to suck your pussy?" He walks closer until his face is inches from my center. He licks his lips and studies the throbbing of my clit. His eyes flick to my face as I hold myself up on my elbows, watching him.

My hair is fanned over his bed as he kneels between my legs waiting for my answer. "I'll lick, and if you tell me to stop. I will."

"Okay."

He lowers his lips and licks. I lift my ass seeking his tongue when it retracts. He groans and I moan on contact. He quirks a brow. "More?"

"Yes," I say, breathlessly.

He smiles and slides his tongue inside my pussy and fucks me with it. He licks and sucks and twirls as I moan.

"Dravin," I call out. "Mmm, Dravin."

"That's it, my Raven. Call my name, baby," he rasps against my clit. I grind on his face, and he uses the tip of his nose to swipe my clit, and the tingles cause my pussy to pulse all over his face and lips, and I scream. I can't take what he is doing. I lay flat on my back and he pushes his face deeper. He groans against me. He licks his lips and stands.

He flips me so that I'm on all fours and eats my pussy from behind, sucking my puckered hole, and I turn my head and watch as he fucks me with his tongue.

"Oh. My. God."

"That's right, baby. I'm your God. This pussy is mine. I'm going to fuck you and suck this pussy until you can't scream my name anymore."

Oh my god. My body feels alive, and I need him to fill

me. I raise my head, and the words that have been stuck in my throat slide out of my lips. "Dravin?"

"Yes, baby."

"Please."

He kneels on the bed, and I feel the mattress dip from his weight. He lowers his pants, and I feel his cock rubbing against my thigh. He knows I want him inside me. I can't help myself. I want him to erase all the hurt. I want him to tell me it was a cruel joke or something other than the gut-wrenching feeling of him hurting me the way he did.

He slides the head of his cock inside, and then he pounds into me. He fucks me and fucks me, and I break like he promised. I explode from the orgasm that rips right through me. The slapping of skin and the moans escape my lips as I come. "Dravin," I gasp.

"I know, Raven." He slams into me and hot cum swirls inside me, filling me. Branding me. His cock pulses inside and I arch my back so he can fill the deepest part of me. His grip on my hips is firm as he holds me still until he is spent.

He pulls out slowly, and he slides his hand around my waist up my torso pulling my back against his chest. His mouth is in the crook of my neck. "I'm never letting you go," he whispers.

I close my eyes, turn my head, and place my lips on the side of his head to breathe in his scent. "Then don't," I respond.

He turns me to pick me up like a bride and carry me to the bathroom. He places me in the shower and turns on the water. It is so different than the first time we had sex. He's different. My eyes follow his movement, and I watch as he makes sure the water is at the right temperature before turning on the rain shower. He grabs my hand, pulls me toward his chest, and rests his chin over my head. "I'm sorry. There is a good reason. I promise. I thought I was doing the right thing, but I wasn't. I was hurting you. I was hurting us."

I don't know what he means. He regrets what he did, but why does he keep saying there is a reason—a reason to keep me safe? I don't get it.

He washes me just like the first time. Except this time, he sits me down in front of the vanity and brushes my hair. He then blow-dries my hair until it's smooth and flowing down my back. He gives me a grin, which I see when I look at his handsome face in the mirror. It is the most intimate thing to have a man blow-dry your hair.

He moves out of the bathroom and returns with a silk robe. "I bought this for you. I hope you like it. He pulls it off the hanger and holds it open so I can slide my arms through the sleeves.

He grabs my hand, kisses my fingers, and closes his eyes like he is afraid I'll disappear. My feelings for him are all over the place. One minute, he makes my heart soar, and the next, I'm afraid. I'm afraid he will finish breaking me and I won't survive.

"Come, I need to show you something."

I nod, and he sits me on his lap in front of his massive computer. He tells me about The Order, how it all began, how the university is built around the church, all the things he shouldn't do, why he claimed me, and why he did what he did.

"I did make a bet with Veronica, but I don't want her. I didn't know you. I never thought you would be this amazing person, that you would be my Raven. I'm sorry for everything, Gia. Please. I need you to understand that I'm part of this, and there are people who don't have good intentions."

"Like everyone."

"Yes. Like everyone."

"So what now? I'm considered Prey or whatever. What does that mean for me?'

"A Prey can choose who she wants to be with. It's not like when you're married. Once you're married, the man chooses how he wants to lead his marriage. Faithful or unfaithful, she doesn't have a choice."

I swallow and look at Kenyan's history, his family tree, and the major players—basically, the major players controlling the economy.

"What happens if they don't follow the rules?"

He looks at the computer screen and leans his cheek on my side. "They die."

My eyes widen. "They what?"

"They die, Gia. The Order decides when and how to get rid of them."

"Have you?"

He nods, "Yeah."

He knows I'm asking him if he has killed people. If he has had to. I close my eyes and shiver.

"Are you cold?"

"No. I'm scared, Dravin. I'm scared for you, and I'm scared for everyone."

I hear a knock at the door. "Are you two done bumping uglies or what?" Valen teases through the door.

Dravin rolls his eyes. "What am I going to do with that knucklehead."

"Punch him in the face again to make the other side even."

"Not a bad idea."

He taps me on the thigh. A signal for me to get up. I tie my robe around me to make sure I don't flash my naked flesh to Valen as Dravin yanks the door open and Valen almost falls inside.

He laughs, but Dravin doesn't laugh with him. "What do you want?"

Valen's eyes gleam with amusement when they land on me in my robe. "You kissed and made up." He gives me a wink.

I roll my eyes, crossing my arms over my chest. "What?"

He shakes his head. "Nothing. I can see it."

"See what?" Dravin growls.

He smirks at Dravin. "How madly in love she is with you."

I avert my gaze because I thought I could keep my feelings hidden from everyone. I tried to hide it, but Valen could see it.

"Dravin's eyes caress me and then turn dark when they land on Valen. "Your point," Dravin snaps.

"I just thought you should know," Valen answers. "It's written all over her face every time she looks at you. You better do something about that. Or…they will."

Now that I know what he means, another thought pops into my head. Jess.

"Does Jess know?" I ask both of them.

"She knows enough now—not like what I just told you, but enough. She is safe from the others for now."

"He means as long as we keep fucking her," Valen drawls with a knowing gleam in his eyes.

We, meaning both Reid and Valen. I wonder how Reid feels about that, but then again, it's not my business as long as Jess is safe and happy.

CHAPTER THIRTY

GIA

IT IS THANKSGIVING BREAK. Jess went to her family's dinner, and I had to fly out to meet my dad in his new house with his new girlfriend. My mother is already there. I'm dreading being in the middle of this awkward dinner and can't wait to leave and I haven't even arrived.

Dravin has been the sweetest and most amazing in bed. He hasn't let me go back to the dorm. He wants me in his house, preferably in his bed. We sit and do our homework together, watch movies, and binge on TV shows like a real couple. I haven't brought up the order, the rules, or even our relationship at this point. He made sure all pictures and comments about what happened were removed.

The argument I saw him having with Veronica was about her sneaking into his house and being a psycho bitch, posting that about me on the school's social media.

The Uber drops me off at my father's now larger home. This is the first time I will meet his girlfriend and my stomach is in knots. I look up at the medium-sized home with a three-car garage and notice it's much newer than the home I grew up in.

When I approach the walkway, the white front door opens, and my father appears.

"Hi, sweetheart. I'm glad you could make it. Your mom is inside with Carolyn." My father greets me.

I place a small smile on my face because what daughter wants to spend Thanksgiving with his father's new girlfriend that he cheated on your mother with. Oh, and my mother, too. This sucks.

"Hi, dad." I greet him in return, giving him a hug.

I walk inside the warm house, the smell of turkey and homemade pie in the air. I can hear voices coming from the kitchen. One I recognize as my mother, and the other must be Carolyn. Another voice is of a man.

"Oh, Carolyn wants you to meet a friend of hers from work. He is about your age and couldn't' spend Thanksgiving with his family."

I smell a setup. My father has been worried about me dating because my mother had me raised in a bubble practically my whole life. I'm not sure she would approve of the way I have given myself to a broken man who is part of one of the richest organizations in the world. If my parents only knew I'm attending a school full of sinners.

"I'll take your suitcase upstairs and put it in the spare room."

"Alright," I tell him, removing my scarf, gloves, and jacket.

I told Dravin I was having Thanksgiving dinner with my parents, but I didn't know how to ask him if he wanted to come or if that was something I was supposed to ask. I hate labeling what we have because it is so complicated. Sex is the only thing not complicated between us, but I have hope. You can't help who you fall in love with. I just hope he feels the same way. He said he was going to visit his father, so I held my tongue, but I didn't have the courage to ask him to come with me. In all honesty, I was a little worried he would tell me no.

I walk into the kitchen, and I raise my top an inch above my breast because the guy who is watching from the corner has his eyes aimed right at my chest instead of my face. His brown eyes scroll over me like he is undressing me.

"You must be, Gia," he says, walking over. He has sandy blonde hair, his dress shirt rolled over his forearms, and khaki slacks. He looks like he just got off work and didn't have time to change.

My mother, Laurie, gives me a small smile and looks over at a petite woman with brown hair and a big smile. "You must be, Gia. She comes up and gives me a kiss and I stiffen.

"Hello, everyone." I nod toward my head. "Mom."

"We are so glad you could make it. How's college life treating you? Your dad told me that you were attending Kenyan. That is very impressive."

"Yeah, wow. Very impressive. What are you studying? My name is Colin, by the way. He holds out his hand." I give him a normal handshake. "Gia. I'm studying economics."

"Very, cool."

Economics is not cool, but whatever. I guess Colin is just trying to be nice.

"How about church." My mother chimes in.

"Laurie." My father walks into the kitchen. "We discussed this. No church comments while Gia is here. This is her senior year and she is on her own living on campus at an elite university. I'm sure there are better topics than church to talk about. She has gone to church with you every Sunday since she was practically born." He chastises my mother.

"Fine," she says in a clipped tone, giving me a wry smile. I'm sorry."

"Don't be sorry, Mom. I went to confession and attended."

She gives me a beaming smile. If she only knew the priest wasn't a real priest and real sinners are the ones that go every week.

I feel bad my father embarrassed her, but I can't say I'm not glad. Everything about my mother is regarding church. She has this thing with it. She should have just joined a convent and devoted herself to God. She would have been happier, in my opinion.

I clear my throat.   "Do you need me to help with anything?"

Carolyn shakes her head. "Oh, no. I've got everything under control." She gives me a wine glass with some white wine. "You go with Colin to the living room and chat for a while.

Colin takes that as an excuse and grabs a beer. He waves his hand for me to go first. "Ladies first."

I walk ahead of him praying he isn't checking out my ass. I take a seat in the living room and notice that my father has pictures of him and Carolyn everywhere. I even notice one they took together while he was still married to my mother. Prick.

"Is this your first time meeting Carolyn?"

I'm annoyed because he damn well knows the obvious.

"Why don't you ask me something that isn't stupid."

I know I'm being a bitch, but come on, first, he undresses me with his eyes without even knowing my name, then he asks me stupid questions he already knows the answers to.

He places his beer on the coffee table. "Alright? I know you don't have an official boyfriend or anything. How about you go out with me tomorrow? I want to ask you out on a date. How does that sound?"

I'm about to turn him down when the doorbell rings. I look over at the front door. "Are we expecting company?"

"Not that I'm aware of. I work with Carolyn, and she didn't mention anyone else stopping by."

My father opens the door and I hear the voice from the last person I expected. Dravin. I stand and watch as my father's eyes widen at an impeccably dressed Dravin with perfectly tailored slacks and a black dress shirt with a grey embedded pattern under a long overcoat. His hair is neatly trimmed. His driver comes into the foyer and drops off three designer suitcases.

I tighten my hold on my wine glass. He greets my father and shakes his hand.

Carolyn's voice can be heard from the dining table. "Dinner is ready, everyone," she calls out.

"Honey, I think you need to set up for one more."

My mouth goes dry when Dravin looks up. He turns his head when the driver hands him two bouquets of flowers— one of black roses and the other of different colors.

"Thank you," he murmurs to the driver. Then he says something, and the driver says, "Of course, it will be delivered, Mr. Bedford."

My father raises his eyebrows, turns to me, and tilts his head toward Dravin. My father looks over at me and mouths, "Wow," silently.

"Who is that?" Colin asks, his voice low.

Dravin walks further down the hallway in my direction. "I hope you don't mind me showing up beautiful, but I missed you already."

Oh my God. He is just perfect. My mouth breaks into a smile. "Never," I answer him softly.

He hands me the black roses and I place my nose inside and smell them. He leans in right when my mother and Carolyn walk in to see who showed up taking my lips in a passionate kiss. His hand cups the side of my cheek and I melt into his embrace not caring if we have an audience.

"Oh, my," Carolyn whispers.

"Jesus," my mother says.

My father clears his throat.

"Everyone. This is Dravin. Gianna's boyfriend from school."

My eyes find his and he leans. "Is that ok?"

I nod my head vigorously my eyes turning glassy. "Oh, yes."

His eyes move away from me and land on a speechless Colin. "Hello, I'm Dravin, Gianna's boyfriend. And you are?"

"Colin," he says.

Dravin gives Colin a once over then looks him square in the eyes. Dravin has two inches on Colin and has a bigger build. He gives Colin a *she's mine* stare down.

I fidget with the hem of my top and Dravin's eyes trail over the slight swell of my breasts. "Are you trying to spoil my dinner, gorgeous," he teases.

My face heats and I look over at my mother. "Mother, this is Dravin."

"I see that, sweetheart." She turns to me. Now I know what to call him: boyfriend. "You attend Kenyan also?"

"Yes, ma'am."

"Oh, please call me Laurie."

"Alright, Laurie. Yes, I attend Kenyan with R-Gianna." He clears his throat. "Forgive me, but I tend to call Gianna my Raven."

"You are so well-mannered, young man," my father says.

"Thank you."

Carolyn claps her hands. Well, dinner is served and welcome, Dravin. I'm thrilled you could make it. I notice she gives Colin a sad smile. I knew it. It was a setup. That was why he was quick to ask me out and why he looked at me like I was dinner. Let's just hope he behaves.

Everyone takes a seat. Colin tries to sit next to me, but Dravin moves quickly and raises an eyebrow. "I think your seat is over there." He points across to the other table.

Dravin removes his coat and unbuttons the first two of his dress shirt and rolls up his sleeves.

"Eyes over here, honey," my father says to Carolyn, whose eyes widen in embarrassment.

My mother raises her eyes and scans Dravin's arms and neck, no doubt inspecting all the ink. Even Colin notices and looks nervous.

I rub my lips together because it is rather intimidating. Dravin is not a small man, and with all the tattoos, it can be overwhelming if you're not used to them.

Carolyn smiles and waves a fork in Dravin's direction. "Are those everywhere? Don't they hurt?" she asks. I almost choke on my wine.

Dravin looks at me to make sure I'm not choking. When he is sure, he turns to Carolyn.

"You mean my tattoos. Is that what you're asking."

"Yeah. I'm sure her mother is wondering the same thing. Right, Laurie?"

She licks her lips and gives me a small smile. "I—

Dravin interrupts her. "They are." He looks over at me and licks his lips seductively. "Gianna knows where they all are."

"Oh my," my mother says softly.

My eyes find my father, but he keeps opening his mouth and closing it.

"Gianna, how are the dorms? Is everything okay?" My father finally asks.

He hasn't called or visited, so I wonder why he cares. I

tense and place my fork more forcefully than necessary in my turkey, showing how I feel about the matter.

"I remember when I was in college three years ago, it was the luck of the draw who you got as a roommate. You're lucky you only have one year left," Colin says before I can answer.

My eyes lift and Dravin meets my gaze. He turns and his attention lands on my father. "She doesn't have to worry about living in the dorms or her tuition."

"Oh, and why is that?"

"Because I have made sure it's covered, and she doesn't have to share a dorm room."

"Where are you staying, sweetheart," my father asks me.

I swallow the food in my mouth forcefully.

"I'm staying with Dravin."

My mother drops her fork. "Excuse me?"

My eyes land on my mother's appalled face as she looks at me and then to Dravin and back.

Colin leans back and smiles. "As roommates?" he interjects.

Dravin takes a sip of his wine and bobbles his head from side to side. "If you call her sleeping in my bed roommates, then yeah, I guess we're roommates," he says with a smile.

"Gianna!" my mother screeches.

I roll my eyes slightly. "Yes, mom."

"How dare you?"

Carolyn looks at my father and then to me. "Laurie, relax. You are overreacting. She is a grown adult, and she can date and do…other stuff."

"She is well taken care of."

"Yeah, in your bed," she snaps.

"Mother," I scold.

Dravin scratches his brow with his forefinger. "I'm sorry,

but it makes sense. Gia told me how you feel about the church and your religious views."

"What happens when you're bored of her, huh? Where will she go?"

My stomach clenches because my mother has a point. What happens when he gets bored of me and wants someone else? I lower my gaze and fidget with my hands under the table. This is not how I expected Thanksgiving to go.

"I assure you she doesn't have to worry about that."

"What will you do for money?"

Colin snorts because he figures Dravin lives in a small apartment, barely making it by like most typical college students.

"What do you do for money, son? You seem really sure of yourself. Colin understands the struggle. He owns the brokerage firm Carolyn works for and how hard it is to get started when you graduate college. How hard it can be to stable enough."

"Daddy, please."

"Honey, give him a break," Carolyn tells my father.

Dravin pinches his nose, and I know he must be annoyed by everyone.

"I have and make enough."

"What is your last name, son? Let's start there. Who are your parents?"

"My name is Dravin Bedford. My mother is dead, and my father is very much alive. I'm one of the three founding sons of Kenyan."

My father's eyes widen, and Colin almost drops the mashed potatoes. "You mean to tell me I have a billionaire's son or maybe a billionaire sitting at my dining room table?"

"Yes, sir. That is accurate."

"Y-you're a Bedford," My father stutters.

"I'm well aware. Like I said, Gianna lives with me on my estate off campus and she has her tuition paid for in full."

"Holy shit," Colin whispers. "You're like one of the richest families dating back generations.

If they only knew he was part of the most dangerous and corrupt organization ever. He's part of The Order and eventually one of its main three. Now, he's my boyfriend, and he wants me for himself.

My teeth scrape my bottom lip, but Dravin places his thumb to keep me from committing damage. "Easy there, gorgeous. I wouldn't want those pretty lips to sting."

Colin puffs his chest out. "Could I get a picture taken with you?"

"As long as Gianna is next to me," Dravin shrugs his shoulders and gives him a predatory smile. Why not?" Dravin leans closer over the table. "Keep your eyes on my girl, and all will be good."

Colin blinks multiple times, like something is stuck in his eyes. "I-I'm sorry. I-I didn't know."

Dravin points with his wine glass in his hand toward Colin's nervous face. "That's your only warning," he says on a chuckle.

Is Dravin jealous? Dravin's hand slides under the table, and he places it possessively over my thigh and gently squeezes it.

"Honey, you have that boy wrapped around your finger," Carolyn says, as if Dravin didn't just threaten Colin.

CHAPTER THIRTY ONE

GIA

I WAS SURPRISED my mother and father didn't object when Dravin placed his bags in the guest bedroom. One of the bags he brought was full of designer clothes he purchased for me, with the option to return anything I didn't like. He wanted me to have new clothes to wear for my trip to see my parents.

Where this version of Dravin came from, I have no idea, but I want him to stay with me forever.

"Are you ready?" Dravin asks.

I check myself in the mirror for the tenth time. I am wearing a black wool dress with sheer black pantyhose and an overcoat with matching leather boots. I decided to wear my hair down and light makeup. Dravin is wearing his overcoat since the temperatures have dropped significantly. He looks handsome in his all-black attire standing behind me. We look striking together. Together, I love the sound of that. His eyes hold me through the mirror.

"There is no emptiness or lies inside of you. Your soul is not on the other side, but *with* mine. Always."

He kisses me on my cheek and murmurs, "You're forever mine."

My stomach flutters and I turn and tell him, "I love you."

He smiles. "I know."

He doesn't return the same words. I'm not sure if I should feel sad or happy. I close my eyes and he squeezes my hand.

"Let's go. My father is waiting."

We are having dinner with his father, and I'm nervous.

Extremely so. I wonder what he will think of me. Am I good enough? I'm also curious as to why he came all this way to have dinner after Thanksgiving and not during.

The sports car that was delivered to my father's house is something straight out of a magazine. The doors lift up, and I'm instantly surrounded by warmth. He has the car warmed up.

"Thank you."

"My pleasure."

The restaurant is a nice venue in the city. It is discreet, expensive, but small. I have the feeling the restaurant was chosen, so this could be a small affair.

We are ushered to a table where a man with a medium-sized build and eyes dark as night is seated. He looks like Dravin but slightly older. He is still handsome for his age. I could see myself with Dravin in the future. It gives me a glimpse of how he would look when he is his father's age. Still as handsome. You can tell by the way the waiter keeps giving him appreciative looks. The other patrons glance over at Dravin and me with curious stares as we make our way to the table.

"Why are they staring," I whisper to Dravin.

"Because you're beautiful, Raven."

Mr. Bedford watches Dravin remove my coat and tilts his head, studying me.

"She's gorgeous, son. I can see why you picked her." He turns to me. "Please, have a seat, Gianna."

Dravin holds out my chair and I carefully take a seat then watch him sit to my right. "Thank you for the invitation."

"My pleasure. You're here so we can discuss your relationship with my son."

I stiffen and my eyes lift to meet Dravin's hard ones. He

obviously doesn't agree with his father, but I want to know what this is about. Is he warning me off? Is he trying to tell me I'm not good enough because I don't have money or come from a wealthy family?

"Okay," I say softly, placing my hands on my lap. My appetite quickly vanishing.

"I know you are aware of how things are done, but my son brought a stipulation to my attention. I can only allow it if you agree. You have to be willing."

Dravin is quiet and he leans back in his chair. Waiting.

The waiter brings food we never ordered, but it all looks delicious. Dravin begins to eat like this is a normal conversation. I'm not sure if this is customary when his father is present, but the self-assured guy from yesterday is gone at the dinner table. He is this silent spectator, not voicing a word.

"Willing to what?"

Mr. Bedford's eyes darken like a man possessed by something evil.

"Breed."

My eyes snap to Dravin.

My nostrils flare. Did he just say what I think he did? Breed? I'm not cattle.

"He means have my child," Dravin says softly. My heart softens and my anger slowly lifts.

My brows pinch, and I realize that he hasn't been using condoms anymore when we have sex, and I'm not on the pill yet. I went to the doctor to get it, but I need to wait until after my next cycle to start. Dear God. Is he? He wouldn't?

"When the time is right and when I'm ready. I can see Dravin and I having a baby someday," I answer.

"My son has to marry before he graduates, and you are his choice. The only way a girl from your side can be with him is if you fall pregnant. Once the child is born, then you can get married. When you marry, all the rules will apply as if you were married in an alliance.

He means because I'm considered Prey, they have to make sure I can give him an heir to keep the order going. If not, he has to marry someone else.

"If I don't."

"Then he keeps fucking you until he is done with you, but he will marry who he needs to marry. You can always be his mistress. It isn't uncommon, and faithfulness isn't required in our relationships, whether we are married or not. This is a chance to change your life. You will want for nothing. The decision is up to you."

My head whips to Dravin. He lowers his gaze. "Is that what you've been trying to do? Get me pregnant?"

He doesn't flinch when he answers. "Yes."

"Why?"

"Because you're mine."

CHAPTER THIRTY TWO

GIA

I DIDN'T SPEAK to Dravin after having the most strenuous dinner with the father of the man I have fallen in love with, who can also flip on me and make me miserable for the rest of my life. He wants me to breed like a cow right after graduating college and be married to a man who doesn't have to be faithful if he doesn't feel like it.

"I'm sorry, Raven," he says after I walk out of the bathroom, getting ready for school.

"Sorry?"

"Yes, I'm sorry. I don't know how else to keep you."

"Keep me." I snort. "I'm not a dog or a bird you can put in a cage, Dravin. I know you are part of this secret cult thing, but how am I supposed to accept it? No matter what I decide, I'm doomed to a life of hell."

"How is it a life of hell if we are together."

"Because how will I know you won't cheat on me? How will I know you are faithful when you don't have to be? It's a life of slavery."

"You sound like—" He trails off.

"I sound like what?"

He takes a deep breath and looks up at the ceiling. "You sound like my mother did when she was alive."

I stop moving and peer over at his pained expression. I don't know what to do—choose him or not choose him. He can say everything is great, but once I'm tied to him, I lose all ability to do what I want. My child is then thrust into this society of sinners. Is that what I want? Is that what is good for me? For us?"

I walk up to him and wrap my arms around his waist. His arms wrap around me, and I'm swallowed inside his embrace. I lean my forehead against his hard torso.

"What would you want?" I gaze up at him. "What do you truly want?"

"I want you."

"You have me."

"I want you to have my child. I want you to be mine."

"I'm scared. I'm so scared."

He swallows and looks down at me. "I know.

I sigh, "What if I can't get pregnant?"

"You were just checked. Don't take the pill, please."

He went with me to the clinic to get on birth control. I didn't want to ruin our relationship with an unplanned pregnancy, but I never thought that he was actually checking to see if I could have children. I should be upset, but I understand why he did it. He was trying to find a way to keep me in his situation. For there to be an us.

I huff. "Easy for you to say. You're not looked upon like cattle."

He laughs and it's the most welcoming sound.

"The last thing I think about when I look at you is cattle," he rasps.

My lips seek his, and we kiss until I'm almost late to class.

I walk toward the cafeteria. I still have the meal plan from the beginning of the semester, so I make my way over. Maybe I'll get lucky, and it will be empty. I'm walking in, and I find Jess with Valen, but there is no sign of Reid.

"Hey. What's he doing here?" I point to Valen.

Jess swallows the bite of what appears to be a sandwich. "Hi. Um, Valen was just sitting with me."

He places both elbows on the table. "What's wrong? I can't sit with Jess now."

I take a seat next to Jess. "I didn't mean for it to sound like that. It's just that you're usually with Reid."

What I was trying to say is that I thought Reid was into Jess and not Valen. He seems the playboy type, not the serious type. He's a sophomore with two years to mess around and live carefree as a college boy. I know Jess has had sex with both, and that is her business, but she's my friend and I'm still going to look out for her. She's Prey, and people have already taken advantage of her.

"It's ok, Gia. Valen was just leaving."

He lowers his elbows and leans across the table toward Jess and lowers his voice. "Think about it." He gives her a wink. "See you later."

He gets up and looks down at me, wearing his fitted shirt and jacket. Valen is a very attractive guy, and girls break their necks to get a glimpse every time he passes by the same way he breaks their hearts.

"You're a good friend, Gia. She's lucky to have you. Just so we're clear, I kinda like Jess."

My eyebrows shoot up. Did he just say he's interested in Jess? My head leans in, and I try to rile him up the same way he always does to me. I bump my shoulder against Jess. "A lot of people like Jess. She's hot."

His nostrils flare. Like Dravin, he loves a challenge, and if he truly likes Jess, this is my way to make sure he treats her right. I know the rules, thanks to Dravin, and he knows it. He knows I have to make a decision regarding Dravin and our future. I can easily be part of The Order if I want, and not just by being with a regular member. I will be at the top as the future wife of one of the founding members.

When Valen walks away with a scowl on his face, I turn to Jess and ask, "What was that all about?"

"Valen being Valen. Don't worry about it. He plays around a lot. It's hard to tell when he is being playful or serious."

"What does Reid say about the way he acts around you?"

She takes a bite of her chips, and you can hear the crunch when she crushes them with her teeth. She's thinking about her answer, or maybe she just isn't sure.

"I don't know, and honestly, I don't trust guys. Especially guys from this school. Dravin is the exception because he cares about you. He moves you into his house. He treats you like a princess. I could go on. The man is batshit crazy, head over heels. I'm not sure I'll ever have that."

"I don't know what to say to you other than that you have a choice, Jess. Believe it or not, we do."

She slides another chip in her mouth. The annoying crunch bouncing in my ears. "My choice is to not give in to any of them. I've been treated like shit before, and I won't do that again, ever."

"What do you mean?" My stomach clenches in worry. "Did someone hurt you, Jess?"

She laughs but not the kind of laugh that makes anything that was said funny. "Let's just say I have trust issues. The whole thing with Garret put the nail in the coffin. I'm in college and will have fun like every other college kid my age. I know some don't agree with the things I've supposedly done, but I have my reasons, just like they do. Emotion is not part of it, and I'm ok with that. If they think they're emotionally unattainable, then they don't know the meaning of the word."

When she says they, I know she means the guys who are part of The Order. Maybe she can find a nice guy like Marc or someone who isn't part of The Order—someone who goes to a different school or something.

"How about dating someone from Ohio State, like that guy Dillion? He seemed nice."

She snorts. "Reid almost killed him. I don't want to be the cause of some poor guy disappearing."

Cold dread snakes up my spine because I know they are capable of it. Just because I haven't seen it, doesn't mean it can't happen.

I slide my hair to one shoulder and let out a frustrated breath. "Fine, I get it, but promise me you will be careful. I mean... screw what anyone thinks. Just be careful."

She drapes an arm around me and smiles. "I know you're just looking out for me, and I think you're an amazing person." I smile, but it is wiped off my face when Warren saunters in and stops at the table where we are seated.

"Hey there, gorgeous." He sits down next to me, and I notice his cast is off.

"What do you want?" I snap.

He raises his hands up in mock surrender. "I was just being nice. I have never been anything but nice to you."

True, but he gives me creepy vibes almost all the time. He always looks around like someone is going to pop out and catch him doing something he isn't supposed to.

"Why are you here?" I ask.

He glances at Jess and then at me. "To give you a heads up." He nudges his head toward the doors leading to the hallway on campus. "See for yourself."

Then he gets up and walks away.

Jess's eyes follow me as I get up and make my way to the

hallway, pausing when I see a girl placing her hands on Dravin's chest and giggling. His face is emotionless, but he doesn't do anything to move her hands from where they are planted. My eyes sting and my throat feels like it closes with the searing pain. My vision narrows like I'm going in and out of a tunnel. My mother's words at Thanksgiving instantly hit a deep part of me that I refused to consider a possibility because I wished that what we had was strong enough for him to be different.

Will I always have to wonder?

What if he gets bored and tired of me? I will be trapped with no way out. My eyes begin to fill, and my nose gets clogged with unshed tears.

The brunette fondling my boyfriend must be a member because she isn't in the dorms, and I've never seen her in the cafeteria or anywhere the Prey usually hang out. Her clothes are definitely upscale, and she has a perfect figure. I'm sure she is a better fit to be with someone like Dravin. She leans up to say something close, but he turns his head to listen. When he turns to get away, he stops when he sees me standing by the door leading to the cafeteria. He swallows and then looks at the girl who has a triumphant smirk planted on her face.

"Please don't let me interrupt," I say, turning and walking away.

"Raven!" Dravin calls out. "It's not what it looks like."

"I'm sure. It seemed like a lot what it did. I was standing there for a hot minute. Look, I gotta go," I tell him.

He grabs my hand. "No. Please. Let me explain."

I pull my hand out of his grasp. "Explain what?" I snap. "That it was a mistake. That it's not what it looks like. Let me guess: She was lost, and she happened to find her hand on your chest after something funny you said. Wait...let me guess, you've slept with her already. I bet my life on it."

His eyes dim, and I know I hit the nail on the head. He's fucked her. It doesn't matter. If it's not her, it will be another and another. Then I'll turn into one of those jealous psychos that can't cope. I'll be a nag which will result in him doing the one thing he is notorious for doing, screwing whoever he pleases. Either way, same result.

"I'm sorry. I know I have a past, but that was nothing. I don't want her."

I snort. "Well, it sure as hell looked like you wanted her." My eyes lock on his and he grimaces when he sees how hurt I am. I have to set aside my love for someone who has never told me he loved me. I have to set aside the attraction. I can't think about his gorgeous face, his perfect body, and the way he makes me feel when I'm in his arms.

All the times I dream of happily ever after.

All the times I picture the child or children we could have together.

I wonder all the time what it would be like to be by his side or married to someone like him.

It would take a split second for him to destroy it.

Like a ruined castle crumbling to the ground, I'm at the bottom with my heart in my hands, praying to be saved.

"Raven, please look at me."

My eyes find his, one light and one dark. I decide. I decide what is best for both of us. I would rather he be a stranger and me a memory, than be cut open and bleeding for the rest of my life.

"I'm sorry, Dravin. I can't. I'm so sorry."

"No, please, baby. I'll make it right. We can go home, right now. We can talk about this. I promised I wouldn't."

He promised he wouldn't be unfaithful, but my father vowed the same thing to my mother, and look at how well that turned out.

I laugh ironically. "Yeah, I can tell. What would happen if it was the other way around, huh? The shoe on the other foot."

He clenches his teeth, and his hands turn into fists. "There would be a body to be buried."

"Huh, I guess I should go and get a spot in the 1918 section, or should it be in the late 1800s."

He raises his chin. "That could be arranged if that's what it takes."

I snicker. "I don't think there will be enough space in the cemetery to bury all the bodies."

He gets closer, and his fingers touch the tips of my hair, curling it around his thumb. "I'm not giving up on us. I won't."

"I don't know. I just need time. This is all too much right now, Dravin."

CHAPTER THIRTY THREE

DRAVIN

I'M WALKING down the hallway when I spot Jess. She slows down and I quirk a brow.

"What?"

She takes a deep breath because she knows I'm on edge. My Raven is distant, and she is closed off. That stupid girl, I can't even remember her name, was trying to get me to screw her or test my loyalty to Gia. Some people can't fathom my love being for her and only her.

It is a hard decision to give up everything to be with someone like me, who is part of a secret society with rules we only follow.

"I just think you should know that it appears that the whole scenario that played out in the cafeteria was a setup to get Gia to break it off with you."

I begin grinding my teeth because whoever is behind it, is dead. No question.

"I'm listening."

"Warren came to us when we were sitting at the cafeteria and acted like he was being a friend and looking out for her best interests. He told her to go see what was happening outside. It just so happened it was at the exact moment what-ever her name is, was chatting you up."

"It was a setup so she would break it off with me. Then she would be vulnerable, and he can swoop in and be her hero."

I curl my lip in anger. My left eye begins to twitch

because he's done. Order or no order. She's mine. No one gets to hurt her emotionally or physically. She means that much to me.

"Yeah, I think that sums it all up. I also wanted to warn you about him." My eyes follow the way she fidgets, and a nagging feeling snakes up my spine.

"About... It's ok. You can tell me."

"I-I don't like the way he looks at her. I know it doesn't make sense, and no one picks up on it, but I do. I just want her safe, but Warren is... Warren."

"I see. I'll take care of it. If you need anything, you can come to me, and if you don't feel comfortable with me, Reid, or Valen, tell Gia, and she will come to me."

She swallows nervously and averts her gaze to the wall. When someone has been in pain for so long, they can see it in others, and in Jess's world, there is plenty of it.

"Okay," she whispers.

I sidestep and walk past her into my favorite class because it's with my Raven and I can write about her.

My eyes meet hers, and I smile, yet it falls because she seems defeated. One of the girls I have slept with gives me an appreciative once-over. I roll my eyes and make my way to Gia.

"You look better every time I see you, Dravin," she purrs.

I ignore her and see Gia's eyes flash in anger at her. I instantly regret every woman I have slept with before Gia. I hate that I cause her to feel uncomfortable. I look over to Rebecca and then Gia and say loudly enough for everyone to hear.

"I may have slept with many women, but I've only taken *one* to my bed, and that is the only place that matters. You are the only woman that matters. They are my past, but you are my present and will always be my future."

My Raven looks up with a slight grin on her lips and tears in her eyes. I give her a wink and take a seat right next to her.

The professor walks in, and class begins. After thirty minutes of a lecture on literature, he faces the class behind his podium.

"If you don't mind, Mr. Bedford, I believe you are one of the few I haven't called upon to read your latest entry.

I pull out my notebook and flip it to the last page and read.

I am lost like the forgotten footprints in the snow. Yet, you stand like the fire against the cold. Like a dark Raven bringing light, guiding me to you so I can hear the silent whispers of your soul.

"Very deep. Very deep." He glances at Gia, just like everyone else in the class. "You must be his Raven."

"She is," I say quietly.

The professor's eyes land on me, giving me a curt nod. "Understood."

He knows what it means. That she is mine in every sense. I know it, The Order knows it, my father knows it. Even Rebecca lowers her gaze. They know that in this moment and from now on, Gia is untouchable. I have claimed my Prey.

CHAPTER THIRTY FOUR

GIA

"WHAT'S WRONG?" Jess asks me. We are back at the dorm after a full day of classes.

"I need to talk to you. I need to talk to someone, but I don't know who to talk to."

Jess gets up and gives me a hug, wrapping her arms around me. "What's wrong? Gia, tell me. Did something happen? Did someone hurt you?"

"Yes, to the first and no to the second," I sniff.

"What's wrong?"

My eyes close and tears escape running down my cheeks. "I'm pregnant," I blurt in her shirt, making a wet spot.

"What?"

I raise my head and sniff. "I'm pregnant."

"Shit," she mutters.

She sits down on the edge of her bed and holds her curls tight on top of her head. "Yeah, I get it. Double fuck." She lifts her legs, crisscrossing them, and pats the bed so I can sit beside her.

I sit and rub my face with my forearm. "What am I going to do?"

"First off, are you sure? These things can be false positives, you know."

I pull the paper out of my coat pocket and hold it up. It is from the clinic.

"Blood doesn't lie. I started the pill, but I was too late. I wanted to give myself time but didn't think, so now I'm done."

"Done? No way. You have the hottest guy on campus who is crazy in love with you. He's a little off and intimidating but rich as fuck, and you have his kid growing inside you. It's a win-win in my book."

"Yeah, you forget that he is one of the sons of The Order."

"Yeah. I get it, but—"

I interrupt her. "It means I have to marry him, and he controls my life. If he wants to cheat on me, he can, and I can't do shit about it. He can do whatever he wants. I could be his slave and I wouldn't have a choice. They have everything at their disposal. Even if I move to Greece to escape them, I'm sure they have a member there, too. They're like the fucking Illuminati."

"That's a myth, by the way."

I raise my hands and place them on my head. "Yeah, but these people aren't, Jess."

She lowers my hands and places them on my lap. I wipe my face with a tissue she picks up from the tissue box. I sniff and take a deep breath to calm my nerves down. I've been feeling emotional and crappy. I have mood swings and the smell of certain colognes make me gag—except Dravin's. His scent calms me down, if anything. It is like the child growing inside me recognizes him and knows.

"You need to tell him, Gia. He needs to know."

"I know, but I'm afraid."

"Don't be. He will be happy."

"But I have a feeling the others won't be. Like, Veronica."

Jess snorts. "I'll handle that bitch. Trust me. She has bigger things to worry about."

"How's that?"

"That's another story."

There is a knock at our door, and I try to quickly compose myself while she opens it. When she opens the door wider to see who is standing there, I sigh in relief. It's Reid.

"Hi," he greets Jess. He peers in from the doorway and sees me. I give him a watery smile. "Hey, partner."

His eyes narrow because he sees me crying. "Tell me," he says in a stern tone.

"It's nothing."

He points and looks at Jess. "Tell me," he repeats.

"She pregnant," Jess blurts.

I lay flat on the bed with a thud. "Thanks a lot, blabber-mouth. Now he's going to run back to the fort and tell the puppet master."

Reid walks over and looks down at me with a knowing grin. There is something different about the way he is staring at me. My heart beats wildly like when a cat catches the mouse or the tiger pins down the gazelle. He tilts his head and looks down at my stomach, then picks up the paper I have clutched in my hand and reads it. His eyes scroll through the test results. He chuckles like in a horror movie, and Jess looks at him like, *what the fuck.*

His dark eyes meet mine, and he says, "Welcome to the Order."

The End

Want a Sneak Peak of Lust Book 2 of the Prey Series on the Next Page.

Want a sneak Peak of the Circle of Freaks by my Alter ego Delilah Croww?

An excerpt can be found after Lust

Please Note: Delilah Croww books are for readers with no triggers.

Signed copies and book boxes are available at carmenrosales.com

SECRETS ARE KEPT.
GAMES ARE PLAYED.

LUST

CARMEN ROSALES

CHAPTER ONE

GIA

When Reid found out I was pregnant, he made me feel very uneasy. The emotion that crossed his face as he saw me crying sent shivers down my spine. The kind of shivers you feel when watching a scary movie and you can imagine what the starring characters are going through.

Reid walked closer, watching my tear stained cheeks, he smiled sinisterly and gave me the expression of a man that is hiding a secret about the future. Like a predator that hasn't shown its true colors, and it's too late to walk away after you're caught in a cage.

So I assume they all take their Prey seriously. Dravin explained to me the ways in which the Order exerts its influence to achieve its goals. The basics of it all, but I know there is more. He was just brushing the surface.

When I open the door to leave the building, a blast of icy air rushes in, and I wrap my winter coat more tightly about me. Temperatures are dropping and the thought of my unborn child causes tears of unease to form in the back of my eyes. Where have I gone wrong? You'd think a guy like Dravin would try his hardest to prevent me from falling pregnant so soon. I know it's also my fault in not taking the proper precautions even if he is what I want for my future. You can't help yourself when you fall in love. It blinds you when you're trapped in the feeling. That person is all you think about. He becomes the first thing you think about when you wake up and the last person you think about when you fall asleep.

They become everything. They consume every waking moment. He consumes every waking moment.

To this day, I still remember what Dravin's dad had to say about raising a child that belonged to Dravin, but I didn't think he meant right now. When he said "after graduation" I assumed he meant somewhere in the far future.

To be honest, at first, I thought a guy like Dravin would lose interest in a girl like me. I love the flowers, the letters, and the sex. What girl wouldn't and obviously from the attention he gets around here, I'm not the only one who would have fallen for him or has fallen for him.

I'm scrolling through my phone to order a ride-share when I hear the rumble of a motorcycle getting closer. I look up and it's a black-and-red sports bike coming toward me, the exhaust causing a small cloud of smoke against the cold air. The rider is wearing all-black gear and the helmet is also completely black, including the visor. My heart begins to race as the rider revs the engine.

I raise my shoulders at the piercing sound as it assaults my ears. The leaves that have fallen from the trees are scattered around from the force of air emitted from the exhaust. The biker is riding on the walkway, not caring if it leads into the building.

After a few seconds, the rider cuts the engine and I take a step back, not knowing who is riding the powerful bike. Instead of going back inside the building into safety, I stand there frozen, not moving, wondering whose face is under the helmet. His body is completely covered, not giving anything away, and I can't help but be curious.

On careful inspection of the bike, it resembles a professional racing motorcycle. The kind you see on TV in Europe. Since the rider's face is obscured by the helmet, I have no idea who he is but it is obvious that the rider is male based on the sartorial choice of jacket and trousers, which are tailored to fit over wide shoulders and powerful thighs.

I take a deep breath and try to move away from where I am staring at the unknown rider, but my legs are immobilized. I ignore the chill in the air as I watch the guy place his feet on each side of the strong motorcycle between his knees, then take off his gloves. As I release my breath and look down at the tattoos on his knuckles, I recognize the tattoos across the skin of his hands when he pulls the last covered finger. *Dravin.*

"What are you doing here? I was just about to go to your house."

He takes off his helmet, his hair tousled, but he doesn't care; in fact, he probably wouldn't care if it were sticking up in a funny manner. Dravin always looks amazing, no matter what he wears or how he wears it. Some people are just lucky that way.

He looks directly at me, and his attitude is gloomy and impenetrable. An odd feeling snakes up my spine. There are times he acts different around me. Quiet. Reserved. Like he is watching me. Studying me. I'm not always sure he's the one who's been sending me letters and flowers. It's as if he were two distinct people in one package. He baffles me. As much as he piques my interest, he terrifies me. Sometimes.

"Are you sure about that?" he asks.

I nod. "Yeah, where else would I be headed to?"

He holds his helmet and gives me a side grin and chuckles, folding his arms over the gas tank of the bike and turning his head in my direction.

"What's so funny? I need to talk to you. It's important."

I want to snap at him, but I know it won't help him listen

to what I have to say any better. It's unclear how he'll react to the news. How angry will he be? Disappointed? Tell me to go fuck myself. Be happy.

"What do you need to tell me that you're running off at sundown alone looking for me at my house without calling anyone to take you?" he scolds.

"What I have to tell you cannot wait," I retort.

The trembling spreads to my hands, and I release a puff of air through pursed lips, mimicking the appearance of smoke.

My hands keep trembling, and he picks up on it. A tense shiver can fool him into thinking it's the weather outside, but the truth is that I'm rather anxious.

What's the best way for me to break the news that I'm expecting? I did the math and I won't start showing until after I graduate, which is why I really don't want anyone to know about it.

Because it would officially initiate me into the Order, I had no intention of informing him until at least a month later. In case I miscarry. I read that first time pregnancies could end up as a miscarriage.

Initially, I was hesitant to be with him because he belonged to the Order, but then I remembered the baby. It's too late. I'm too late to make that kind of decision. Not because of the baby but I love him. I'm in love with him.

"Get on," he says in a stern tone.

"What?" I ask, shaking my head. He can't be serious. I have never been on a motorcycle before. I shouldn't because of my condition but it's not like I can blurt it out right here. Right now.

"You heard me. Come here." He waves at me with his helmet for me to step closer.

When I walk up, his eyes roam over my jacket. "Zip that up and let me place the helmet over your head," he instructs.

"I don't know how to ride, and I don't think I should," I say instead. I can't break the news to him right now, in front of the dorm hall.

Watching him on his motorcycle reminded me of the day I first arrived at Kenyan and saw him for the first time. He was holding a helmet while pointing me in the right direction. It was obvious he rode a motorcycle, but the helmet he was holding at the time was different.

After I zip up my winter jacket like he instructed, he places the helmet over my head and fastens the chin strap. The helmet is a bit loose, but he fixes the problem and opens the visor so I can see his eyes. One light and one dark.

He motions with his fingers to the right side of the bike. "You see the pegs?"

I nod, breathing in the scent of his cologne that is coming from the pads inside the helmet. His voice sounds muffled because of the helmet padding against my car and I take a deep breath and listen to his instruction. You would think it would smell of sweat but it smells of ocean breeze and him.

"You place one foot on each side and you wrap your hands around my waist and do not let go," He instructs. "Make sure you keep your hands on tight, alright?"

"Okay," I say, loud enough so my voice doesn't sound muffled.

Once he places his gloves back on and fires the engine revving the gas, the sound is more bearable with the helmet on. I place my right foot on the peg and hold on to his shoulder, swinging my leg over the back seat until I'm fully seated.

He slides his leather gloved hands over my fingers that are locked over his leather jacket at his waist.

He caresses them and I like the feeling. The feeling of being this close to him wrapped around his body. My spine is tingling with anxious anticipation when he turns the key in the ignition and starts up the bike.

As soon as I hear the click of the clutch, I brace myself since he is shifting gears on the motorcycle. Shortly after he sets foot on the road, I open my eyes and see the road underneath us, like the massive belt of a running machine.

The asphalt on the road is going at a breakneck pace. He's not reckless but traveling fifty mph on a motorbike is different than doing so in a vehicle. Every one of your senses is amplified, and you feel every gust of wind and bump on the road. The only things that count are your emotions and the events occurring around you at the moment. I can simultaneously hear the machine whirring between my legs and feel the firmness of his muscles as I lean against his back. As if there is no separation between us. Danger right below but safe above having him in my arms.

After ten minutes, I glance to my left and see that we are no longer on the street where Dravin lives. He takes a corner into a street I'm not familiar with, but I can see immediately that the homes there are grander and more spacious. Partially obscured by tall gates and high walls.

A greater sense of foreboding as we pass each gate. These residences are more like estates, complete with massive gates and tall hedges on all sides.

Trees moan and swing as they shed their leaves. My jacket isn't protecting me from the wind's icy sting and I don't feel Dravin tensing up or shivering in the chilly wind, therefore his suit must be designed for this kind of weather.

I'm relieved when the black iron gate swings open toward him as he slows down, and he waits until there is enough room for the bike to pass through without having to wait for it to completely open. The sting of the chill was quickly getting to me.

A dark-gray stone walk leads to double doors of a house that gleam gold from their windows. The outside wall sconces give forth the same warm light as the inside ones, but they are powered not by bulbs but by fire. To my right are six black garage doors.

After the left garage door is entirely open, there are seven more bikes in a row. Different brands and models with their beautiful paint jobs glistening beneath the glow of the garage lights.

He taps my leg, which I take to be a signal to get off, and then he extends his arm out, palm up, to help me maintain my balance as I swing my leg over.

Once I am on solid ground, he drives the bike forward and parks it inside, moving the kickstand with the heel of his boot. My eyes look around the massive house taking it all in.

Once the engine is switched off, the stillness engulfs me. The silence mixed with a small ringing in my ears from the loud bike. He walks over to where he left me standing, the sound of his boots over the cobblestone driveway, watching me fumbling with the chin strap.

His gloves are removed and his warm fingers glide over mine and undo the strap. He squeezes his fingers over my freezing hands and his lips curl down into a grimace.

He quickly lifts the helmet off my head and my hands fly to pat down the strands that stick up, running my fingers over the long tresses of my hair, noticing they are slightly knotted from the ride over but not too bad.

I'm about to ask him whose house this is, when his voice floats back over from placing his helmet on a shelf in the garage. "Let's get you inside. It's getting too cold out here."

"Where are we?" I ask.

He looks around, and his countenance is unsure for some reason I can't quite place. Something seems off with his attitude. In some ways, it is him, but in others, it isn't. To me, he still looks the same. He has the same gait, but a very different demeanor.

The Dravin standing before me is not the Dravin I know; he seems to be possessed. In my opinion, this is not the same Dravin I fell in love with. This is a rare side of him I've only seen a few times, but trying to get to know him better, I didn't give it much thought. I constructed the reason for his actions in my mind as him coming to grips with the evil that lurks within him. There is clearly something sinister inside him, if I had any doubts before. Something about him appears threatening. Dangerous.

Looking at his brighter left eye, I see that the right one is as dark as a storm at sea. It reminds me of the moment before a thunderstorm breaks out when the first black clouds roll in and the lightning strikes the water. Illuminating the dark depths.

He leans in toward me, his gaze fixed on mine. "You said you were on your way to my house." He points to the entrance. "This is my house."

Incredulity makes me raise an eyebrow. *What the fuck?*

My throat clears and my chin goes up. "You know the house I was talking about. Stop attempting to screw with my mind; I have no idea how many homes you have. You should have said something if you're in a grumpy mood; then I wouldn't have gone with you when I could have gone back to my room."

His face breaks out in a broad smile. I feel him come closer until his lips are almost brushing mine. He examines my top lip before moving on to the rest of my face and then my jacket.

He's on the cusp now bringing our lips together, I need only sway a centimeter for our lips to connect. Damn him. He makes me weak. When I'm with him, I totally lose my sense of reason.

"You know what I meant, Dravin," I whisper.

The tip of his tongue peeks out of his mouth. He tilts his head like he is going to devour my lips in a single kiss, but he doesn't. "You're right. I am in a mood, but it has to do with me not being inside of you. I want you on my bed with your legs spread out while I decide which way I'm going to fuck you with my tongue and then how I'm going to feed my dick to your pussy."

The movement of his thumb causes my chest to rise and fall. My thighs clench trying to catch the drip of my arousal as it slides down my thighs while the cool air fans the heat breaking out all over my skin.

His thumb pulls my bottom lip, exposing my teeth. "Such a pretty mouth. There is nothing I want more than to keep you in my bed."

"I am in your bed. I practically live in your bed."

I'm more in his bed at his house than my own dorm room. Sometimes, I miss Jess, but then Dravin is inside me, filling me. Making me forget that I'm in college and that it's my senior year. It's like my future doesn't exist. Only the present. When I'm with Dravin, nothing else matters except us.

"This is my father's house."

He brought me here. Why?

"Why?" I ask.

He knows that I'm asking why he brought me to his parents' house.

His thumb slides across my bottom lip. "Why not?" he counters.

I shiver with eagerness. He brought me here to sleep with him in his bed at this house, but I didn't come with him to have sex. I came to tell him that I'm pregnant.

CIRCLE OF FREAKS

DELILAH CROWW

Ivy Sloan

Since I was a little girl, I fell in love with the circus. It's all I ever wanted to see up close or be a part of. There was no room for things like that where I grew up. There was no room for anything except bad memories and bad expectations.

Every year around Devil's Night, since we moved to Stockbridge, the Circle of Freaks paranormal circus comes to town. It's an eighteen-and-over horror show in which no one talks about what goes on inside because they can't.

But this year is different. This year, my prayers have been answered by gifting me a ticket. Despite what people think of me at school. Despite the girls gone missing—— Found dead. I wasn't prepared for what I would see.
I wasn't prepared for…him.

CHAPTER ONE

I stare at the wall with all the scuffs of dirt that needed paint. The kind you wonder how they got there or if the wall is even worth painting over because it will look the same a few weeks later. I wonder how much longer. How much longer will it be before I get out of this shithole.

When you have money, that wouldn't matter. You would paint it. Except for those who earn a paycheck above poverty —for people like us, that isn't an option. And if you live at the Meadow River apartment complex in Stockbridge, Mass-achusetts. The ones who couldn't pay their light and rent in the same month.

The Meadow River apartment building is old. It still has the box air conditioners that hung out the windows. Some have duct tape to make sure it wouldn't fall out.

According to state law, a landlord is not required to provide air-conditioning. When the summer heat came, I had to walk around half naked. We didn't have enough for the electric bill. Like most tenants living in Meadow River, they had to choose the rent or the air conditioner in the summer.

I pour the last few drops of milk into my cereal bowl. A sheen of sweat coats my forehead. I look at the dry cereal, debating whether to throw it out or eat it dry. I walk over to the sink and turn on the faucet, adding some water into the bowl. Placing it down, I check the time. Ten minutes before the bus pulls out front.

I mix the cereal with water and a few drops of milk with my spoon, close my eyes, and take a bite. It's not the worst I've tasted, but it sucks to eat cereal with water.

I take a deep breath, checking the time again, bracing myself for my last year of high school. Three minutes. If it were up to my mother, she would have told me to hell with it and ask for my hours back at the grocery store. I repeated the eleventh grade because I had so many absences and failed all my classes. I had no choice but to skip school that year and get a job or risk getting evicted. My mother doesn't make enough at the diner she works at, so it's up to me to help with rent.

The kitchen light goes out. I drop my spoon with a clank and open the front door to see if the yellow light in the hallway is still on. If we were a couple of days late paying the electric bill, the first thing I did was look outside to see if anyone else's light was still on. If it's not, it's a blackout. If it is, our light was shut off for non-payment.

Looking up, I let out a relieved breath. It's a blackout. I have to ask my mother if she paid the bill before the shut-off date. If not, we wait until I get paid from work or when my side hustle comes through.

Grabbing my bag and dropping the bowl in the sink, I head out, locking the door behind me. The Meadow apartments aren't bad compared to where I lived my freshman year in South Carolina. This place beats the trailer park filled with meth addicts. This was the best my mother could do, coming from a background of jobless addicts and prostitutes. I walk down the stairs because the elevators are out of order, which is no surprise. They smell like piss anyway.

The obscene graffiti was something that always stood out. It was on the neighbor's doors and the walls in the hallway in big black letters sprayed over the peeling paint. Some were on the elevator doors. No one complained that the building hadn't been painted. It looks like it's been that way since the early seventies. No one wanted the place to look too nice for fear they would raise the rent, and we would all get screwed.

I look at the thoughtful message, SUCK COCK. It has a picture of two big testicles with a gigantic penis drawn above it and, SMOKE AND FUCK. The messages changed every so often. No one knew who did it, and the night security was too busy sleeping on the night shift to give a shit about it. There were no cameras or daytime security. Anyone could come inside the building, which was disconcerting.

The yellow public school bus arrives on cue with FUCK SCHOOL spray painted on the side. The apartment complex is behind the Stockbridge Mall. The drive-in theater behind the mall is called the Coyote Drive-In. The drive-in plays one new release and three classic movies every week.

Stockbridge was founded in the seventeen hundreds. It has old architecture and historic homes on the west side of the school. A fair also opens when it is above thirty-eight degrees in the colder months. Stockbridge High is the middle ground. The center of it all. Where the teenagers meet, graduate, and go their separate ways.

I hop on the bus, ignoring the smirks and stares aimed my way. The bus gets on the highway from the parking lot that separates the plaza from the apartment complex. A forest surrounds the whole town.

The only way to reach this side of Stockbridge is the main highway. It's old, and no one comes to this side unless you live here or want to park to watch a movie or the mall. No one goes to the plaza. Everyone knows that is the last thing people do at drive-ins. It's an excuse to park your car with dark-tinted windows so you can fuck in the back seat.

I should know. It's how I lost my virginity my sophomore year in the back seat of the star quarterback's Mustang. He said the right things to get me to go out with him.

It didn't even hurt the first time, and every time I think about it, I hate myself for being so stupid. I didn't care about losing my virginity. I had to lose it to someone, but I should have done it with someone else. Not a six-foot-two, tanned skin, ash-blond hair, blue-eyed asshole like Tommy Hill.

After reading about how perfect and magical sex and love were supposed to be, I realized how bad at sex he was. A girl like me didn't expect love. Not where I came from or how I was raised. When we moved to Stockbridge, I wanted to fit in. I wanted to experience what I read about, and no one knew where I came from. I thought Tommy was different, and he knew what he was doing since he was so good on the football field. I wasn't prepared for how bad it would be.

I can feel Tommy's hot breath on my neck. He rubs his fingers over my clit to get me wet. His fingers are rough and uncoordinated. I watched enough porn on my piece of shit cell phone in my bedroom to see how it was done. He shoves into me, and I expect a burn from him penetrating my barrier, but nothing—a lot of rubbing and no sparks.

He looks up, and I make the same face I saw the girl getting fucked on my phone. It works. He ate it up.

But it was over before it began.

"Oh fuck. Ivy. You feel so good and tight, baby. Oh... fuck."

I could feel nothing, but he couldn't tell by the fake noises I made.

He grips my legs on the uncomfortable back seat of his Mustang and trembles like he has the chills.

When he's done, he lies on top of me, out of breath, the seat belt buckle digging into my lower back. I feel hot and sweaty. I wince when he goes soft, sliding out of me like a tampon.

"You were amazing. Did it feel good, Ivy?"

I paste a fake smile when he looks up. "You were perfect."

I wanted to cry. I hated it. He plants a wet kiss on my mouth, finally getting off me.

The next day at school, I found out we were both liars, but for very different reasons.

ABOUT THE AUTHOR

Carmen Rosales is a Latinx author of Steamy, and Dark Romance. She loves spending time with her family. When she is not writing, she is reading. She is an Army veteran and is currently completing her Doctorate Degree in Business and has the love and support of her husband and five children. She also writes under Delilah Croww for her DARK romance horror stories with really dark themes. She loves to see a review and interact with her readersJoin her VIP list- www.-carmenrosales.com

.

Scan the QR code to follow her on Social Media, sign up for her Newsletter, and for preorder links for upcoming releases:

Carmen Rosales

Made in the USA
Coppell, TX
04 July 2024